**By**

# Samie Sands

**2014**

**Triplicity Publishing, LLC**

**ISBN-13: 978-0988619692**
**ISBN-10: 0988619695**


Printed in the United States of America

First Edition – 2014

Cover Design: Triplicity Publishing, LLC
Interior Design: Triplicity Publishing, LLC
Editor: Amanda Poythress - Triplicity Publishing, LLC

# Acknowledgements

Thank you to Alea Hamilton and my editor Amanda Poythress – your input has been invaluable. I'd further like to extend my appreciation to everyone involved with Triplicity Publishing, LLC for helping Lockdown come to life.

I'm extremely grateful to my husband, James Sands for his endless patience and support, and to the rest of my wonderful family. Of course, I must also thank my 'zombies' – Jasmine, Oliver, Jordan, Kate, Rhys, Kain, Paul, Tracy, Adam, Alex and Eden – for your remarkable work on the Lockdown website.

# Dedication

To my beloved grandma.
For your continual inspiration.

# ONE

Ok, it's official. I'm dead. I'm actually going to be killed.

Then I'll lose my job, my important position complete with my beautiful nameplate, with *Leah Watton* in shiny silver print. Of course, this will lead me to get kicked out of my flat and I'll end up living in some cardboard box on a skanky street corner, drinking cider and trading war stories around a bin fire.

Or the much worse option, I'll be forced to move back to my parents' house.

Stupid. Stupid. Stupid.

All for one idiotic joke. I can't believe it, I've nearly wrecked my career already, and it was only just beginning. I can really feel the panic welling up in my stomach now. After those three long years at university studying journalism, the thing I was so sure I was destined to do with my life, which in the end turned out I actually hated. Those long depressing months of sending out CV's to every stupid newspaper, magazine and supplement going—my parents had always made it very clear that they expected me to use my degree sensibly, especially as they may have helped me now and again, financially, after I got into a bit of credit card debt. I got rejected time and time again, even by a cheese periodical. Seriously, they said at the interview my lack of passion for the subject was apparent. I mean, what sort of person is passionate about cheese?

Finally I got a chance, well more like a small teeny tiny stepping stone, one that would actually go down well with my family. A news researcher. I mean, it's for the least watched local news program ever, in a small rural part of the country where nothing exciting ever happens, but it totally counts. I was so relieved, but definitely not happy to get this job. Still, I can't afford to lose it.

I'm such a fool. I only did this to impress Jake. Damn it. I've been trying to get his attention since I walked in on my first day and saw him smiling into the phone and twisting his hair in that cute way he does when he's concentrating. He’s absolutely gorgeous—tall, dirty blonde hair, blue eyes, a smile that lights up a room. I was instantly smitten, and have since spent my days catching any glimpse of him that I can.

He definitely likes to think he's the joker in the office, so after spending hours every night trying to plan sexy outfits—which believe me isn't easy if you're 5’3”, with dull mousy brown hair that match your eyes exactly and a figure that could do with losing about 10 pounds—to combine with flirting and trying to seem like a really cool girl with such an interesting social life—none of which caused him to even blink an eye in my direction—I thought I'd try a different approach to getting his attention.

He's one of those guys constantly emailing stupid YouTube videos to everyone, often with a fake news story attached, usually mocking one of our more recent, tedious stories. So I found a great one of a 'zombie' attack. It's brilliant. It looks so realistic and although it's in a foreign language and you can barely make out any words, the narrator sounds terrified. It made me laugh when I found it, and I knew Jake would find it funny, so I set it up.

But then came the error. I feel icy and uncomfortable even thinking about it. I accidentally sent it to Jamie King, the big boss. With a whole bloody news story attached.

He doesn't understand humour and I'm sure he's never heard a joke. He seriously does not tolerate messing around in the office. This can only mean he's either going to think I'm serious and I think this should actually go on television, on the news, like some idiot who doesn't deserve this job, or he's going to see it for the joke it is and instantly sack me. Oh God I don't know what's worse, I can't cope with this.

I'm such a klutz. If I hadn't been talking to Michelle about the new blue high heels I bought at the weekend to go with my black swishy dress, and I was actually concentrating on what I was doing for a change, then none of this would have happened.

She's still talking to me about them now, and about a

night out she's planning for someone's birthday, but I can't focus on a word she's saying. I'm just filling in all the pauses with “yeah” or “oh right” which seems to be satisfying her, for now. She always was the talker in the friendship.

The waiting is almost worse than the inevitable boot. I'm on the edge of my seat, tapping my fingers and shaking my legs nervously. I keep seeing Jamie pacing up and down in his office, but not once has he come into the main room. I'm so scared I could throw up. I can't concentrate on anything. I keep logging onto Facebook just to calm down, which is actually just going to add to my bollocking, I realise as I quickly click on the cross.

Ok this is getting ridiculous now. It's been hours and still nothing. Maybe, he just hasn't checked his email yet, or maybe my ideas are so insignificant he deleted it without even reading it. This idea bucks me up a little bit. In fact, now I think about it, he's been on his phone all morning, chattering away quickly and nervously. He looks really stressed out, and actually kinda sweaty. Gross, I screw my nose up in mild disgust. This man is far too important to be worried about some silly email from little old me isn't he? I start to chuckle to myself. I feel relieved, almost hysterical.

"What's up?" Michelle interrupts my thoughts.

"Oh, er, nothing." I realise I've been laughing quite loudly. My face flushes red and I pretend to be engrossed in a press release on my desk.

God, press releases are boring. If I worked in PR I'd attach some freebies or something eye catching with everything I sent to anyone in the media. Surely that's a way to ensure you'd get on the news? I'd find out who worked at each news studio and send them something they'd specifically like. For example, for me I'd send a nice new bag. Or, no that might be a bit much; maybe some new bath salts or something. If someone sent me that I'd make sure their product or story got on the news, even if it was really dull.

"Leah." Jamie's voice makes me jump out of my seat. Damn, I'd forgotten all about that email for a minute there.

I quickly close down Facebook. How did I end up on that website again? I'm reading everyone's gossip and not even realising it. I walk quickly to his office with my head down. Everyone is staring at me which makes me feel awful. Mind you, if I was sat amongst them I'd be staring at me too.

"Sit." I sit down very quickly. This is the end for me I can feel it.

The silence lasts for what feels like forever.

"I need you to explain this email you sent me."

"Well, it was just a, um, joke really. I was just erm." I can't stop babbling, my heart is pounding and my face is getting hotter and hotter.

"Where did you find the video?" he asks me as if I'm about five years old.

"Um, well, I found it on YouTube. On my own time of course. I was only messing around during lunch, trying to get a laugh, lighten the atmosphere a bit." I let out a strangled giggle; this could not be going worse. "I would never misuse company property. Except, well, the email. But that was just um, I didn't mean to."

"So, it's not something you have been working on for a story?"

"Er no, I don't thinks it's, you know—" Don't say it. Do not say it. "—real?" Damn it! Why would he need that obvious fact clarified?

"Hmmm, well I want you to send me the video link so I can see what it is you lot are really doing when you're supposed to be working." The look he gives me makes me feel about two feet tall.

I'm shell-shocked as I walk back to my desk. What the hell just happened?

"What was that about?" Michelle whispers.

I shrug my shoulders as a confused reply. Jamie is furious. That much I can see. I can't tell if he really wants the link, or if he was just messing with me, trying to freak me out more than he already has, so I'll never do anything bad again. Well, it's working. I think I'd better do what he asked, just in case.

I suddenly look at Michelle's face and realise she's actually pissed off with the fact that I haven't given her any details to gossip about and help pass the day quicker. I feel totally sympathetic, so I fill her in on all the details.

# TWO

The next few days are uneventful, which is such a relief, but I'm still constantly on edge. I thought there'd be some kind of comeuppance from Jamie for committing such a heinous work crime. At one point I even had myself convinced...well anyway, I might as well put it from my mind because everything is back to normal.

As the clock finally hits five on Friday, I stop typing immediately mid-sentence and close down my computer. Michelle and a few others from work including Jake and I are going out tonight for that birthday Michelle was planning. I think she said it's for Sasha from the legal department. To be honest, I don't think she particularly cares who it's for; she just wanted an excuse for a piss up. I need to look amazing tonight. This is my first real chance. The first time Jake will see me out of work, in a relaxed environment and he can see the real, such-amazing-fun-to-be-around me, which he's obviously going to love.

...

This is a disaster. I frown as I look in the mirror. I've tried on at least a hundred outfits, but I think the stress has caused me to gain weight—on my hips of all places—and everything looks weird on me. I've also managed to develop teenager-style spots. People seem to assume that a vegetarian diet immediately leaves you thin with amazing skin. Oh, how wrong they are. How could anyone like me? My hair is limp, my legs are chunky and I can never get my eye makeup to look good, however many times I practice it.

Not a lot I can do now, it's time to go. I end up in the first outfit I tried on, the black dress and blue heels. What a waste of two whole hours. I feel so panicky I need a drink just to steady my nerves. Luckily I've got a little bit of white wine left over in the fridge, I can't even remember when from, but beggars can't be choosers.

Michelle—who looks effortlessly fantastic as usual—and I finally reach the pub where we're meeting everyone, and it turns out we're the first here, so we head straight to the bar and get drinks in. We're just gossiping about the comical new 'super secret but everyone knows about it' hook up between the married anchor girl and the lighting guy—whom everyone had previously assumed was gay—when everyone else turns up. I feel a frizzle of excitement at the possibilities of tonight, and smile.

Everyone is having such a great night. Drinks are flowing and we're all laughing. I've made sure I'm sitting next to Jake—death stares can work wonders. And to top it off, we've actually been having almost-intelligent conversation. I mean, he keeps laughing at me as if I'm joking every time I make, what I think are, insightful comments, but it's in an endearing way so I'm sure it's fine.

For example, the guys were all talking about the budget cuts and how it affects the recession according to the latest reports—I know why do they have to discuss work when we aren't even there? Still, that's what you get for going out with a group of people who only have their job in common. I piped up and said that I thought everyone should stop saving their money and just go out and spend it. Surely, that would get the economy moving quicker, right?

I don't know if Alisha is purposely trying to embarrass me when she laughs and points out that the whole point of the recession is people don't have a lot of disposable income to spend frivolously, but I can feel my face burning brightly. I have had my suspicions for a while that she is also after Jake, so her comment stings badly. Luckily someone intervenes and attracts the attention away from me quickly, so I can sit quietly for a while, trying to regain my confidence.

As the night goes on, after Sasha pukes and bails—typical, it’s always whoever's birthday it is that ends up worse for wear—people peel away and join other groups or simply go home until finally it’s just Michelle, Jake and I left. Last call is announced and Jake starts putting on his coat, making a move to go. Michelle raises her eyebrows at me. I look at her, confused because I'm not really sure what she means, the drink has made my brain feel fuzzy, so she starts mouthing something frantically to me which I don't understand. I suppress a giggle as Jake looks at me with confusion.

Suddenly my brain clicks into place; of course, we discussed this plan only yesterday.

"Oh um, are you getting the bus home Jake?" I question innocently. I'm sure he lives right around the corner from me.

"Nah I don't live far, just a little way down there."

"Oh right." I quickly interrupt. "Me too. I might as well walk with you then, saves us both walking alone," I continue as he goes quiet. Nerves kick in. Oh God what if he can't even stand to be around me long enough to walk home? It's only about 15 minutes away. How can he dislike me that much? Is he trying to let me down gently? Have I been obvious? I've tried not to be too much. Oh God, it's because I'm ugly. I've got that weird kink in my hair at the back, that doesn't go away however much I straighten it, and to top it off I've definitely got an annoying laugh. I can't help these things he must know that. I mean, no one is perfect. How embarrassing I've been trailing around making idiotic attempts at flirting and he—

"Sure. That would be cool." He smiles. My brain has got so tied up in knots I totally forget to smile back.

We've been walking along for five minutes now, chattering effortlessly, and I feel like I'm in a warm happy bubble. This could actually happen. He could actually like me. In fact, I'm almost convinced he does. I know, I know, there are so many complications to an office romance, like trying to keep it a secret—we all know that never works—or being silently furious with each other after a row at home about whose turn it is to do the dishes, or even the awkwardness of breaking up. But right now, in this moment I can't focus on any of the negative possibilities. Only the wonderful romance ahead. I can even see the wedding dress I'll wear. Ivory lace, strapless with a long train and wonderful stiletto heels. Of course, Michelle will be my bridesmaid, she'll absolutely love that.

As we reach my door, I stop thinking. My heart starts to beat so hard I'm sure he can hear it. The flush in my cheeks must be obvious as much as the nervous giggle—which has somehow got more annoying than usual. I can see Jake's lips moving but I can’t hear what he's saying, just the buzzing in my brain. I should not have had that last shot. Then, I start to get the impression something is about to happen.

...

As I fall into bed later, all I can still feel is his warm lips against mine, his stubble against my chin, and the feel of his breath against my cheek. It was such a perfect moment, better than I could have ever hoped for. I feel so happy and relaxed. I can't get this massive smile off my face, it really did happen. Everything in the world is absolutely perfect, nothing can shake this feeling.

# THREE

Predictably, that's when the world crashes around me, and everything goes to hell.

It starts with me being woken up by a shrill ringing, which is totally annoying because my head is banging. I try and ignore it, but it doesn't stop. My body feels heavy, but I know the only way to get a bit more shut eye is to move and locate the source of that hideous sound.

I finally find my phone under my handbag on the bedroom floor, by which point I'm in no mood to talk to anyone. To make it more insulting, it's a withheld number.

"Yes?" I question rudely.

"Are you her?" comes the reply from an unknown voice.

"Erm." I have no idea what is going on and now my head is starting to spin and my stomach is starting to churn. I really cannot handle my drink; I should know this by now.

"You know, the, er, 'zombie' girl?" the deep voice

interrupts my train of thought; the sarcastic tone is not missed.

"Um." Still none the wiser and definitely in no state to come up with a witty reply I just fall into silence.

"Are you the one who found the story?" He asks again. He's not only treating me as a joke, but as if I'm totally thick.

I'm about to rant and rave at him for calling me at some stupid hour, talking to me so disrespectfully, when my whole body freezes. I start to have the feeling I know exactly what this guy is talking about. My heart starts racing as I wonder who this guy is and how he knows.

In my state of panic I quickly hang up the phone and throw it across the room. I run to the bathroom to be sick. With tears sliding down my face and my throat burning, I run myself a hot shower. Whilst the boiling water is pouring over me, my head starts to clear and my muscles start to relax. I can hear my mobile still ringing in the other room, but suddenly it seems less important. Who knows, it could have been someone from work playing a practical joke—that would be just like Michelle—or a wrong number. It could have been anything. It's just the hangover making me panic. In fact, it was probably a dream, just my worst nightmare coming true.

As I'm pulling my clothes on I feel a lot better. I know for a fact I'm being completely ridiculous. I got totally jumpy over something unnecessary and it's making me crazy. Maybe it's this thing with Jake.

The thought of Jake makes me smile and I relive how well last night went. It's what I've wanted for...well it feels like forever, and it didn't take any fake fashion statements or stupid pranks. He just likes me for me. It just took that tiny bit of alcohol for him to realise it.

...

It's my weekend to work, and Jake's too, so I have butterflies as I make my way there, excited at the prospect of seeing him again. And wondering how we'll act around each other. God, I so hope it wasn't just a drunken kiss. He did insist it wasn't when I questioned him last night, and I definitely didn't want to push it and come across as desperate. As I open the office door, I realise my hand is shaking and I let out a nervous giggle to myself. As the door creaks, everyone turns to look at me. I feel my face getting warm as I stumble over to my desk. Jake must have told everyone what happened and now we'll be the office gossip. Damn, I should have mentioned last night that we should at least attempt to keep it private. In fact, the constant scrutiny will probably stop anything from really happening.

I actually start to feel really annoyed when Michelle whispers, "toilets now!" Oh good, at least she'll tell me everything that has been said.

As the door slams behind me, I realise in the harsh lighting that Michelle looks a little wild, as if she's bursting with some news.

"Ok, what has everyone been saying? Is it that bad? I have to quit my job don't I? Damn it, Jake."

Michelle's smile falters. "Oh God you don't know, do

you?" My blank stare must have answered her question because she carries on "The story, you know the one you sent Jamie by mistake. He ran it on the news last night. The news anchor kind of read it as a joke and then Jamie got really mad and starting shouting at him in his ear piece and he got all flustered and said your name, live on the news!" She looks at me as if I don't understand the enormity of being named on the 10 o'clock news. I don't. I mean, it's the local news that no one ever watches anyway. I just feel stunned.

"But why?"

"Well I think he just panicked."

"No, no, no." How can she misunderstand so badly? "No, why did he put that story on the news? I mean it was a hoax. What the hell was he thinking?" I start pacing and freaking out "That's what the phone call this morning was about."

Well Michelle thinks all the attention I'm getting is great. The local papers keep ringing, and we've actually had a call from a national. Turns out more people watch us than we think. Unless some idiot has put it all over YouTube, which would just be typical of my life. Everyone is around my desk, making me coffees and asking me questions about it all. I'm just speaking in monosyllables wondering how I'm just finding out about this 'news story' now.

Actually, thinking about it, we were out. Of course. I haven't watched any TV, or read any papers since last night. Damn hangover. I mean, I don't normally watch the news, or read papers until I'm forced to at work, but still.

I start feeling really claustrophobic, like I need air. A lot of it.

"Everyone get back to work!" Jamie's voice shocks me out of my comatose state and I stand up, almost as a reflex action. Everyone shuffles back to their respective desks, mumbling and talking under their breaths. He stomps over to my desk, but he almost looks as if he's smiling at me. This is definitely a first. "Please follow me into my office." he says very quietly.

I'm very aware of everyone's eyes boring into my back. The air is rife with tension as I shut the door behind me.

"Now," Jamie starts as I sit down still feeling like I'm having an out-of-body experience. "I'm very sorry your name was mentioned on the news. That was a very unfortunate mistake." I can't help feeling everyone is focusing on the wrong thing. "Of course we'll help you in any way possible," I can hear him saying in the back of mind but I just can't focus on the words.

"But why?" I interrupt and immediately freak. I have never spoken over someone like that, especially not a boss. I'm practically known for being a bit of a goody-two-shoes towards authority.

"What do you mean, Leah? Why did I run the story? Have you actually investigated the link you sent me?" He laughs. "It's brilliant."

"It was supposed to be a joke," I trail off feebly. He continues to stare at me and I feel like I have to continue "To, you know, impress a guy." My cheeks heat up.

"Well maybe you should look a bit further into it. It may look on the surface like a hoax, but it's linked to some real scientific research."

Anyway, to cut a long story short, Jamie really thinks there is some zombie virus spreading which could threaten everyone. I mean, he never actually said the word *zombie*, despite the fact that's what my whole email centred around, but from his description that's exactly what it sounded like. I must be dreaming. That's the only conclusion I can come to. Any minute now I'll wake up warm and toasty, if not slightly groggy, in my bed.

# FOUR

I plonk back down at my desk, praying I'll wake up at home. I sip my tepid coffee and try and assess the situation. I feel stunned, there's no other way to describe it. I just can't believe all this is happening to me. I can hear the usual office chatter going on, and I'm sure some of it is being directed at me, but it's all just white noise blending together.

I have no idea how much time has passed. It could have been a few minutes or even a few hours, but I suddenly jump and realise I can't sit here all day, doing nothing. For one, I could end up losing my job. For two, I probably look like I've just come from the nearest insane asylum. I guess everyone has given up on me because as I glance around the room, no one is paying me any special attention.

I really feel like a total fool and I'm worried everyone thinks I'm an idiot. In fact, I'm sure they do. I need to do something, just to make myself feel better. To make myself feel useful. There must be some way I can redeem my reputation.

And then it hits me. It's so obvious what I need to do, I can't believe I've only just thought about it. Jamie is somehow convinced that this crazy virus stuff is real, so maybe I just need to do what he did, and really look into it. Use all of my journalistic and research skills that I'm supposed to have learnt over the last few months. Maybe I can find out the source of all this 'scientific research' he was going on about, and somehow prove it's real. Or at least possible.

I don't really know why I'm the one who has to convince people, I don't even believe in it myself. It was only supposed to be a bloody joke. I guess it's because my name has been intrinsically linked to the story, it's me all the press are coming to for answers. I feel a sense of foreboding as I start typing. I know I'll just be forcing some kind of belief, but I have to do something.

Oh. My. God.

It takes me a while to locate the original link where the YouTube video came from. The website is foreign. It links to all kinds of weird and wonderful web pages and forums. I can't figure out exactly what had Jamie so convinced, all the 'scientific' stuff seems made up to me. They're all calling the virus AM13, and state that it is categorically not a *typical* 'zombification' virus. I was not aware that there *was* a typical 'zombifiction' virus. Damn my sheltered upbringing. This is because the victims don't appear to die before the infection takes over. Their organs, brain functions and nerves just slowly shut down. Personally, I'm not sure how that is different to dying, but hey that must just be me. The diagrams used to show this look just like the ones in school text books, but that doesn't make it real. Anyone can say anything they want on the internet, everyone knows that.

There are a lot more videos and photographs, very similar to the original, showing an 'infected' person either just roaming around in a comatose state, or attacking someone. All really gruesome and some quite graphic. I'm not sure how they achieve the special effects. I would have thought such convincing body parts being eaten or pulled off by someone's teeth would cost a lot of money. Weirdly everything is filmed on crappy hand held cameras or mobiles, but I guess that's the way to make them look more realistic.

The strange thing is so many people are really falling for it. It seems on a lot of the forums set up to warn of the dangers, people are going wild, totally sure that the end of the world is coming and making their completely obscure 'plans' to survive this attack. Of course, a lot of the debates are about why this is happening. Is it religious retribution? Drugs? A government conspiracy to control population? I've been manically scribbling lists of everything I've read. I'm not really sure why, other than it's just what I always do. I guess it's a way of organising my thoughts and formulating some sort of plan.

The survival tips are great. There's a whole thread on what to take with you if you're forced out of your home: medical supplies, weapons, food, etcetera. One on how to defend yourself against the infected. Apparently killing them is the only option. I guess we don't have to worry about the law then? If you let them get to you first and they touch any of your skin with their teeth, you're done for. It won't be long, and no one can calculate the exact amount of time, until you become the same. That's why it's spreading uncontrollably. Spreading so uncontrollably that no one has even heard about it? Are these people insane?

I get totally lost in all this. It's the most interesting thing I think I've ever read. Much better than the usual local police reports or school events that take up my day. It's not because I believe this deadly virus is threatening, necessarily, but because it has inspired so much fear in so many people. It almost seems like a very convincing cult with hundreds of thousands of followers. When I eventually look up from my computer screen, I realise the room is empty and all the lights are off. I do have a vague memory of Michelle saying bye to me, but I'm not even sure if it registered enough for a reply. God I've been so spacey today.

...

As I'm walking back to my flat, I'm still deep in thought about all this. I know it's all fascinating, but I just can't believe Jamie, who is a very intelligent man, full of common sense—that's how he got the manager's position after all—put it on the news. The 10 o'clock news at that. The one that it seems everyone watches.

Well, except me. Actually, that is a good point. I didn't *see* the news segment. Maybe that would help me understand.

I switch the computer on as soon as I get home, even though I have a headache from staring at a screen all day, and find the news piece almost immediately on YouTube. Figures. Wow, it already has thousands of hits and hundreds of comments. Some agreeing with the incoming threat ('thank you for finally putting this out into the public domain') and a lot disagreeing ('wtf is this crazy shit?') As I watch the clip, I realise very quickly how good Jamie really is at his job. I mean, this is a completely bizarre and ridiculous story, but after the blunder—I can almost see it on their faces when Jamie is screaming at them—he's got the anchors delivering it in a really convincing way. Now I can see why he deserves his job.

Ok, I sigh to myself. After practically a full day of research, I can see there's a huge amount of belief in AM13, even from my own boss. But to be honest, it all just seems crazy to me. This hoax was actually massive before any involvement from me, with a lot of copycat pranksters and I may have just accidentally given it the platform to explode.

# FIVE

I can't sleep a wink during the night. I just lie there with my eyes open, thoughts whirling round and round in my mind. I need some kind of plan. I feel like I can't just let this go on the way it is. I kind of know this story won't just drop and go away, especially now there's been so much interest, and if the national newspapers print anything about this, it'll spread like wildfire. It's too much. It's too mad.

Before I know it, light is shining through the curtains. I groan because I know I need to get up and face the music back at work, the place I least need to be right now. I'm positive everyone must be bitching about me behind my back, because that's exactly what working in an office environment is like. I've never been on the receiving end of it, as far as I know, and it sucks. To make matters worse I'm not further along with my supposed 'plan'.

...

I feel all out of sorts on my way to work. I'm so incredibly tired, but my brain is still buzzing. I pass a newsagents and try very hard to simply walk past, head held high, but it turns out I can't resist going in to check. Just for my own sanity, to be absolutely certain that there's nothing about me or the stupid virus.

To my relief there's nothing about it that I can see straight away on any of the front pages, not even the really trashy tabloids that usually pounce on any ludicrous story they can. It's all about some political scandal that I can vaguely remember someone discussing yesterday. With a smile on my face, I buy the first one I grab and also some chocolate. Maybe I don't need to do anything after all. I've just been paranoid, and kind of vain to think anyone would be that interested in me.

I feel a lot lighter as I arrive at work. I really think today is going to be better. The first person I see is Jake across the room and feeling uncharacteristically brave, I walk over to talk to him, to maybe apologise for not saying anything yesterday and try and gain some idea of how he's feeling, but just as I reach his desk his phone rings and he answers it, quickly turning away from me. As I walk back to my desk, gutted and trying to pretend that I wasn't even heading his way anyway, I realise I've not even acknowledged him, or even thought about him since all this craziness started. I've accidentally played it cool which is not like me at all. I just hope I haven't screwed anything up.

The office is soon buzzing with commotion. Even

with skeleton weekend staff, it always seems like a busy hive of activity here. I'm not getting any special attention today which suits me just fine. I'm not really sure if I have a particular assignment to complete, and rather than go and ask Jamie like I normally would, goody-two-shoes that I am, I decide to just try and keep under the radar. I start with all the usual social media checking—for research of course—and when I get bored of this, I open the newspaper I bought. Although these are really out of date in our world, I figure it might just give me some inspiration.

The pages are all full of stuff that I can't even begin to muster up any enthusiasm for. Stories that have been retold so many times from every angle that everyone has lost interest; a footballer's affair, a politician misusing taxes, another food group that's bad for us. Yawn. Suddenly, I come across a very small article, on one of the middle pages towards the bottom.

I don't know what draws my eye to it. Maybe subconsciously I suspect what it's about, or maybe I glimpsed my name, right there in black and white. In a national newspaper, for the whole of the country to see. I hold my breath as I read.

It's awful, so nasty about me. It calls me a 'ditzy researcher' who has conned my boss with a hoax. They actually have a picture of me, taken yesterday on my way home from work. I had no idea I was being followed, or photographed. It's such a bad picture. I look really dopey in it, all spaced out. If I'd known this was going to happen, I would obviously not have worn my blue bobby jumper that makes me look almost homeless, which is made worse by my obvious hangover. It's not very nice about Jamie either, saying he went along with it in a desperate ploy to up our terrible ratings, and now we've lost any integrity we had.

I can feel the heat rising through my body as I throw the paper down. I glance around the room with suspicious eyes, wondering if anyone else has seen this story and not told me. Suddenly every whisper and giggle is about me and I feel claustrophobic. My throat feels constricted. All I know is I have to get out of here immediately, so I grab my coat and run outside the building as fast as I can.

As the fresh air hits my face, I start to calm down. I continue to walk away because I know that setting foot back in that building will result in tears. I've never cried at work before, and I certainly don't intend to start now. I hope Jamie won't be too bothered about me leaving; I wasn't exactly achieving much anyway. I do have to pull myself together a bit though or I'm going to find myself unemployed, and I'm not bloody job hunting again.

I start to repeat the same mantra in my head over and over again, attempting to convince myself. No one cares about some stupid paper; no one cares about some stupid paper. Anyway, most people who read that paper don't even know me. Why should their opinions bother me?

Oh God, what about all the people I went to school with? My teachers, my uni mates, my parents. What if any of them see it? I'm going to be an inside joke forever. I'll never be able to go to any reunions.

I decide the best thing to do is head home and crawl

into bed. I think the lack of sleep is making me take this much worse. A nap could be the answer to all my problems.

...

This is the absolute last thing I need. My flat is surrounded by people, lots of them. What is going on? There must be a fire or something. I start running, panicking. But as I get nearer I slow down. Something doesn't seem right. There's no smoke or flames, and the people outside my flat aren't shouting or worrying. In fact, they're all stood around calmly chatting. I actually think I recognise one of them.

That's when it hits me. Journalists. What are they doing surrounding where I live? Has someone been murdered? I always thought my neighbours seemed like a weird couple, maybe not criminals, but just a little off. Something I could never explain. I might get a good scoop here, something to justify me leaving work early. I'm just going to act like I've been sent here and join in. We're all professionals here, aren't we?

My steps slow down more and more the closer I get. I don't feel like a professional. I feel out of my depth, a fraud. A frightened mouse about to head into a group of hungry lions. I have never done research out in the real world before. That's for the super confident journalists who don't mind asking all the awkward questions.

“Hi.” I try to talk to the woman at the back, to discretely find out what’s going on, without having to ask. She ignores me though. Everyone does. Before I get the chance to speak again, the guy I thought I recognised, Bill maybe, turns around and spots me.

"Oh my God it's you!" he shouts so they all move to face me. Suddenly Dictaphones and cameras are shoved in my face, and everyone is yelling questions at me at the same time.

Everything starts to move in slow motion. I'm frozen in place. How can I tell them I'm not the one they want, I'm one of them, not the story.

*Zombie.*

*Hoax.*

*Failure.*

All these words are being thrown around me. It is me they want. This thought fills me with utter horror. It's that paper, the story. I don't want to speak to them, and certainly not about that. How can these people honestly be interested in this?

My brain begins to unfreeze and I focus on getting as far away from these prying eyes as possible. This is why journalism never truly suited me. I'm not into pressuring people for information—even less so now I know how it feels from the other side. The only thing I can think to do is run, but to where? All I want to do is go inside, and I have a right to be in my own flat, so I push past them to get indoors. It feels like I'm trying to move brick walls. No one wants to move to let me past, why are they treating me this way? I'm going to have to say something, but I know most of the time that only makes things escalate.

"No comment!" I yell. It always seems to work in films, but now I've spoken, the questions get louder and more insistent.

Eventually I can feel my front door. Luckily I already have my key out so I push my way in and slam it shut.

# SIX

I can still hear them outside. Pounding on the door. Shouting. Well they're definitely taking the side of the story in the paper. I'm the idiot that has damaged our show and might lose everyone their jobs. Fan-bloody-tastic. The tears that threatened to start earlier stream down my face as I slump to the floor, right next to the door.

There really is no way this day could have gone any worse.

Once I calm down a bit, I pour myself a glass of wine, just to steady my nerves. My heart is pounding in my throat and I have no idea what to do. I turn the TV on, trying to block out all the noise that threatens to send me spiralling into a breakdown. I instantly realise this is a bad mistake. News program after news program on every channel. I'm sure there's supposed to always be a Soap on at least one station. I just know my name is going to be mentioned, and I can't bear it, but I also can't turn it off. It's as if I'm determined to torture myself further.

Suddenly, I find what I'm looking for. My picture. That God awful photograph and my name. The anchor is talking about me so I pause and sit down expecting the absolute worst, waiting for the awful words yelled at me outside to be repeated. Yet, somehow this doesn't happen. I'm not quite sure what news programme this is, it's not on any of the main channels. It's on a random Freeview one. As I listen to the words spoken, I can't believe my ears. It's agreeing with Jamie, discussing the virus in great detail. I'm not being shown as a deluded idiot, but as a hero for bringing this to the forefront, giving us an opportunity to fight it.

Wow, this show has really done its research. I recognise all of the early symptoms being discussed: acute tiredness, feverishness, sluggish mind-set. They're pressing on the government to come up with a solution. Whoever started this hoax is going to be laughing. Not only did our show play out to their ideas, others seem to be following. Even if most people don't believe it, there is going to be that little niggle of doubt.

Then, with an indestructible air about me, I make a huge mistake and Google myself. Come on, it's common knowledge that you should never do that, isn't it? I cover my eyes and peek through my fingers as the page loads. As I scroll down, I'm terrified.

Well, it could have actually been a lot worse. At least half the pages seem to think I'm great for bringing this story to the mainstream media, which is a lot more than the ones who are criticising me and saying I'm crazy. Although, obviously there was a lot of belief and information online about all of this before any of it hit the news.

I'm very concerned about how seriously people are taking this thing, but I can't exactly write ‘hey guys it ain't real you know?' to the only people who aren't calling me every name under the sun, from 'attention seeking bitch' to 'fucked up loser'. I have noticed people are so kind from the anonymous position behind their computer monitors. When I log onto Facebook and Twitter I have thousands of new friend requests and followers. Crazy considering I never have anything that interesting to say, but it looks like everyone wants a piece of the action, to know what 'zombie girl' has to say. More likely to have more access to abuse me.

People are emailing me all kinds of crap about this, including Jamie who wants me to keep him updated with every new bit of information I find. I think he's forgetting what I said. I wasn't researching this for a story. He's so focused and driven; he often gets like this when he gets his teeth into a juicy story.

One email details the American contingency plans. I have to admit, it's set out very well, it really looks like a Presidential Initiative, but I can't be fooled into thinking this prankster has gotten to the man in charge of one of the most powerful countries. It states that America is in grave danger being so close to Mexico, where apparently it began. They're setting a strict time frame, and putting everyone who isn’t infected, or showing any signs of carrying the infection, into quarantine. A possibility to keep it practical is to keep everyone inside their own homes. The armed forces will be in charge of delivering everyone their food parcels during this time, which is hoping to be two to three weeks, and during this period, they will 'round up' and 'take care' of the infected. No details as to how they intend to do that part, it's all 'classified' which is never good.

I read this very carefully, at first taking it for the joke it is, but soon realising this is a brilliant idea. You know, assuming that the virus is in fact real—which in turn, does make me something of a hero—so on a whim, I email it to Jamie. I know he'll get a kick out of it.

On second thoughts, I don't actually know what made me do that. Am I going insane? I must have gone a bit stir crazy and let this all convince me it’s true. I think it's the prospect of being a loved public figure, rather than a hated joke, which won me over. Jamie's response is predictably very positive, he wants to continue this story and be the leading news channel on it. I think he's hoping, as we were the first to talk about it, we'll get a segment on a national news programme. It'll be awful when it inevitably turns out to be false.

Once the computer's logged off, I feel as if a cloud has been lifted and I've been dragged out of the insanity. Damn you Internet. Allowing anyone to post whatever the hell they want, and so convincingly.

I look at my phone and realise Michelle has been ringing and texting me. God I must have totally switched off the real world. I call her back and she sounds panicked.

"I thought you were really ill just running out of

work likes that, then not talking to me."

We end up chatting for about an hour and it turns out that Jamie has managed to talk everyone around at work and they're almost all on board with focusing most of our efforts on the virus story. She was stifling a giggle when she told me this. I know they all really think it's dumb, but Jamie apparently thinks it might just boost ratings and get us national, especially with all the extra publicity it's generated, which could of course lead to pay rises.

No wonder they're all 'on board' with running the story.

At least I'm not a joke in the office, I guess. I couldn't bring myself to ask what Jake thinks, and Michelle definitely did not divulge the information, so that's not a good sign.

Anyway, I'm not bothered about what he thinks.

Or the rest of them.

I can just picture all the Emails and texts that have been sent about me. Probably saying I'm mental.

And now they all have to pretend to go along with it, like humouring an idiot.

Oh God what am I going to do?

# SEVEN

I wake up on the sofa at about three AM, head pounding, face sticky with tears. I lie there tossing and turning. There's no point in moving and lugging myself up to bed—I'll never get back to sleep, that much I know. I sigh and flick on the TV. The first thing I see is a random, middle-of-the-night crazy chat show, talking about this story again. There's just no escaping it. I'm going to have to move far, far away. I'll have to go to Outer Mongolia, or wherever it is people go to escape the Internet, TV and general society.

I've been lying in a stupor for hours, mind reeling. Even though everyone at work is now 'on board' I bet they all still think I'm a fool. How can I come back from this? Everyone must think I'm a big joke. To make it much more unbearable, it’s not even like I've just embarrassed myself at the office and in front of Jake. I've made a big blunder for everyone to see. And some people believe in it. There are actually people out there in the world, thinking we are in danger of zombies and a hideous apocalypse. Because of me.

Well, maybe not totally because of me. I do think they already thought it was happening, but still.

Zombies are some bloody science fiction, made up thing, there's no way they can be real. I know according to the science experts from the Zombie Research Centre—yep, not kidding. There are people whose real life job it is, to research the ever present zombie threat—say it's not a zombification virus, but I've seen enough B-movie horror films to know that the description fits. Apart from the green skin and the lust for *'braaaaaaaaaaiiiiinnnnssss'*.

I know, I saw all the 'evidence', the dissertations, the photographs and drawings, the interviews from 'victims', in my online search, but come on. There's no way that wasn't all faked. Think about it: ghost films, totally terrifying. Totally believable and also definitely possible. Zombie films, laughable. They don't even use the Hollywood budget to make them look realistic, because they aren't. No one would ever be fooled.

...

I don't even consciously decide not to go into work for the next week, I just don't leave the house, or even get up. I've stopped answering the door and phone after the first few times. It was just journalists anyway. People I didn't want to talk to. I've cocooned myself inside my house, blocking out the outside world. I sort of worry I'm starting to develop agoraphobia, but I know I can leave whenever I want to. I'm just waiting until all this blows over. I suddenly realise I'm nodding emphatically to myself as I think this, trying to convince the one person who doesn't believe me.

Me.

I do notice in my self-induced madness that Michelle hasn't tried to ring me. She's supposed to be my best friend. I would have thought out of everyone, she would be the person to care. If it was the other way round, I would have been texting her and calling her constantly, checking on her and keeping her up to date on exactly what is going on. Not that I really need her to do that, I can see for myself how much the story has gathered momentum.

The details about the virus have become more explicit and delivered from very reliable sources in a very factual manner, as if it's just a normal thing. Doctors, scientists and other 'leading experts' have been giving out constant warnings of what to look out for, saying to get to a hospital immediately if you or anyone you know displays even the tiniest symptom. Better to be safe than sorry, right?

Most of the 'symptoms to look out for' are obvious. They always zero-in on these. Anything flu like of course- colds, fever, nausea, sickness, that type of thing. Plus stiffness in joints or aching in muscles, and feelings of uncontrollable rage. Apparently, if you experience any of these you must avoid all contact with others and head straight to the nearest hospital, where specialist wards have been set up.

Smaller indications are: odd sensations in your fingers and hands, stomach pains, fuzzy head, dizziness, headaches, tiredness, knee pains, bad indigestion sensations, numbness in your feet or legs. The list goes on with many other unusual and inventive things. These mean you need to get to the doctors, who will assess if you need further examination. I'm sure this is just so every single person will get themselves checked out at some point. The hypochondriac in people will react badly to these vague instructions.

The email I sent to Jamie detailing the 'quarantine' idea is being concentrated on, which is just something else I can take the blame for. The media are really leaning on this and trying to get it to happen. The idea of locking all the safe people indoors for a couple of weeks while they sort out all the ill people is apparently very appealing. I wonder if it's the thought of a legitimate holiday from work. I can see the logic behind it, you know, if the virus is really spreading in the threatening way it's being portrayed. It would prevent the infection from getting to everyone. Also, if people refuse to take themselves to hospital, the only people they will put at risk during the quarantine is their own families.

From what is being suggested—never clearly stated I notice—they're going to give medicine to the people in the early stages of infection, keep them in the special hospital wards for monitoring, and hopefully clear it up quickly. The people who are further along—again, how this will be determined is unclear—will be taken to a specialised medical facility to look after them in the safest environment, while they work out a cure. Which I can only assume means they'll be subjected to humiliating and painful tests and experiments.

As the days of reporting have gone on, it seems to be simply assumed that the quarantine is going to occur. The question changes from 'What are they going to do?' to 'When is this going to happen?' According to statistics, at least 35% of the world's population will die from AM13. Then again, I'm sure they said all this kind of crap about swine flu, and that turned out to be nothing, so I'm not exactly panicked.

The more I watch, the more I think, if they're going to follow through with this whole quarantine idea, then I need to get the hell outside this flat. It's ok staying inside by my own choice, but if it's going to be forced on me I'll go insane. I even have an intense desire to go home to see my family.

No, I couldn't possibly. That would just be madness. I'd worry the hell out of them. The ironic thing is it really doesn't seem that long ago all I could think about was avoiding losing my flat and being sent home. Now all I want is to be back there.

But then again, it has been months since I've seen them, and all this does put things into perspective. 35% is a lot of people and what if...Screw it. I'm going.

I start randomly throwing things into a bag, while I formulate a plan. First, I'll head over to the office, apologise and sort things out with everyone, clear the air a bit. Then I'll hop on the train back to my parents' house. I just need to see them. I smile to myself at the thought of my mum and dad. I know they'll be surprised I've come, hopefully pleased. My younger brother Felix is 17, at the age where he's too cool for me, but I know deep down he'll be happy.

And, you know if I get into work and they tell me it's all crap and none of this is really going to happen, well I can't really face coming back here, it seems too quiet for me now. I've been inside these four walls on my own for too long.

I'll just figure something out.

# EIGHT

The first person I see is Michelle, and she immediately runs up to me and grabs me into a hug, almost knocking me backwards. I have to catch my breath afterwards, she's practically winded me. She's chattering really excitedly at me and I can't follow a single word she's saying. Soon she drags me to her desk, still babbling.

Then she absolutely blows me away by showing me everything she's done. No wonder she hasn't called me, she hasn't had any free time. She's been working her arse off proving 'my' theory right. I'm trying to ignore the fact that even my best friend is referring to this nonsense as my idea. It is nice that she's trying to show the world I'm not a fool but a genius. It's her who has done practically all the research to find out everything that I've seen on the news, plus she's been motivating everyone else to work hard. On top of that, she's been working really closely with Jamie to get fantastic 'breaking news' information which has caused the story to look credible.

Now I can totally see why it's being taken so seriously, despite the fact it's all crap. I'm totally engrossed in everything she's showing me, and her super-fast chatter, like she always does when she's excited, is telling me every detail of what she's been up to; from drafting all the relevant data and getting 'experts' involved, to speaking to MP's and other members of parliament about all the contingency plans. She even appeared on a chat show, trying to ramp up the public approval for the quarantine idea. I'm so gutted I missed that, Michelle is made for TV and she's so charismatic, I wouldn't be surprised if she has a huge fan club now.

From the way she's talking, she actually sounds as convinced as Jamie by AM13 and the threat that comes with it.

"Wait, so this is no longer a joke, you are totally and utterly sure this is real?" I laugh.

"Yeah, I told you we were all on board." She looks confused. "When Jamie talked to us and showed us everything, we could see how real this is. I mean, look at the all the evidence, the new specialist medical facilities being set up. That's not all for nothing. And the videos. Oh my God, the videos. The brave people, risking their lives filming the horror to warn others."

It turns out I totally misinterpreted her on the phone. They really do believe in this madness. I'm speechless. I only have to look around the office to see that everyone is hard at work. No attention being paid to me. I don't think I've ever seen everyone concentrating this much.

Then my eyes lock with Jake's. He smiles at me and I

can't help beaming back. Relief floods through my body. It doesn't look like I've ruined everything after all. Maybe when all this has blown over, we can go out on a real date. As I look at him more, drinking him in, I notice he doesn't look quite right, very pale and ill. He looks like he's shaking and he's got massive bags under his eyes. Flu symptoms. I wonder if he's been to the doctors. I go over to see if he's ok.

"I've not felt great since all this kicked off. I actually think I'm just nervous about it all. Wow that's not very manly is it? It's just a bit mad." He lets out a bit of a weird noise—I think it's supposed to be a laugh.

I think that's the moment I truly realise what an impact this scare is having on people. To be this frightened seems totally bizarre to me, because I'm still not convinced in any way. I just can't see how on earth this whole virus/zombie deal is really happening. Maybe everyone has just got the online crazies, like I had the other night just from looking into it too much. It's so easily done. I just give Jake a hug, having no idea what to say, then head over to my desk.

Before I even sit down and switch on the computer, I notice there's a note from Jamie sitting on my keyboard. It could have been there for days, but it just tells me to go and see him. I guess I should face the music early and get my bollocking over and done with. I can't even begin to imagine how mad he is over me missing such important days of work. Then again, I'm just going to anger him further when I tell him that if this shit is really happening—I of course mean the quarantine not the zombies or whatever the hell they are—then I'm going home to my family, so HR will need to put it down as holiday, if that's even how they'll deal with it. Who knows, I don't think it's something any company is prepared for.

I knock on the door and am instantly ushered to sit down. Jamie is beaming from ear to ear and the praise starts quickly.

"This has been so great for us. Our ratings have gone through the roof. I don't know if you've seen but we've had a small segment on the national news." I guess my days off have not been too devastating to the company then. "We now have more credibility and respect than any other news programme. We found this story and we were brave enough to put it out there." I have no idea what I'm supposed to say, which seems to becoming quite normal for me, so I just nod. "Everyone has been working round the clock to ensure we're always first with the information."

I know if I don't interrupt now, I never will "So, this quarantine. Is it going to happen? It's not just crazy rumours spiralling?"

...

I walk out of Jamie's office in a daze. Apparently 'my' brilliant idea, however much I insisted I found it online, has led to some fantastic plans being made. It is definitely going to happen, they're just working on finer details, logistics and practicalities. After I asked all my questions and sort of got my head around the idea, I told him I needed to go home to see my parents. The simple shake of his head told me all I need to know. He said it's impossible. When it all happens, we're all going to be locked up here, in the office.

Apparently, they're going to set up beds in the canteen and install everything needed to make it feasible. He wants everyone to be here to keep on top of the news. How typical is this, national disaster and I'm one of the unlucky ones that still has to work. We're going to broadcast throughout and be the first ones to keep the UK updated on the progress, on any plan changes and to let everyone know when it's safe to go outside again. He reckons it'll be no longer than a fortnight.

I've spoken to some of my colleagues about it, trying to be discreet, and the shocking thing is they all seem to think it's a great idea. At least we won't be alone, as most of us live in our first flats since our parents, we'll have something to keep us busy and there will definitely be big pay rises at the end of it. I guess that's true. The company will be much richer and we'll have to get some of the benefits, wont we?

Most important of all, we know we'll be safer here than at home. We found the story, there's no way the office won't be protected. It's already behind a wall and you need a pass to get through the gate. We've seen enough of the footage to know that the victims of the virus are enraged, uncontrollable, violent and don't think twice about attacking others, which is the main way it is supposed to be spreading, so in theory we won't be subjected to any of that first hand.

# NINE

The only person whose smile didn't quite reach her eyes when talking about being stuck at work for a couple of weeks, was Michelle, so I called her as soon as I got home.

"Well?" Silence. "What do you think about all this nonsense?"

I'm still thinking hypothetically at the moment. There's no way this is really going to happen. It's not even practical. I mean, they can’t really force everyone to stay indoors can they? Surely there's some kind of human rights act or something that prevents it. Or worse, will everyone be forced to stay in work like us? Oh God this is a nightmare. I actually feel worse about the whole thing than I did this morning, when I was basically ignorant.

To cut a very long story short, she absolutely hates the whole thing. She may have been integral in instigating the quarantine idea, but she did think that we would be given much more choice. She genuinely believes it's essential for our safety and to wiping out this virus quickly and efficiently, but doesn't want to be at the office any more than she has to be.

A lot of people at work deep down feel exactly the same as Michelle, but the extra money is just too tempting. It wouldn't even be a one off bonus; it'll be a permanent raise. And just think how good it'll look on everyone's CV. They're just concentrating on the long term benefits and what they'll be able to afford with all their extra pay to get them through it all; holidays, mortgage payments, new cars. I can totally see their way of thinking, a couple of weeks fanning the flames of fear, then boom. Better career and more money.

But I'm trying to think realistically, what is going to happen when it’s all wrong, that all the information has been faked and AM13 turns out to be nothing more than a 14-year-old boy’s practical joke? And what if, on the crazy notion it is true, what if we're locked up for longer than two weeks? How is that going to work in any practical sense?

I think back to my enthusiasm to go and see my family this morning. It's still there, burning ambers underneath the surface, but I can't do it. If I go to see them, I'm accepting that the government—who I'm assuming are all intelligent men and women—are going to go through with the plans. Which, in turn, means I’m kind of accepting the virus is real?

I've already gone nearly six months without seeing them, what are a few more weeks? I can still talk to them on the phone whenever I like, and I can go and visit when all this has blown over. Assuming we'll have the freedom to make our own choices by then of course. That way they'll actually have reason to be proud of me and my successful career. Hopefully.

And then the urge to stop thinking and get on a train overwhelms me. I've always been weird with superstitious things like this. Like when the end of the world was coming along with the end of the Mayan calendar. I spent the weeks leading up to it telling everyone it was madness and all the people falling for it were idiots, then when the time came around, I had to phone everyone I could think of, just to tell them I love them, just in case.

Full of indecision and a cold unsettled feeling in my stomach, I flop down on the sofa. I know I can’t just sit around doing nothing, that's kind of what got me into this mess in the first place. Well, it didn't help the escalation anyway. I need to decide if I'm going to carry on doing what I'm told by Jamie, or if I'm going to do what I want and risk losing my job.

God this is hard.

So after giving up and going to bed, which is just bloody typical of me, I'm full of restless sleep and nightmares. I wake up in such a foul mood it's incredible, but hardly surprising, considering.

Getting into work does my mood no better. Everyone is just carrying on as if all this nonsense is normal. Why are there no whispered conversations by the water cooler, slagging off the bosses’ new, mad idea? This office isn't normal, I swear.

Delivery men traipse in and out all day, bringing in little crappy camping style beds. It's like I've stumbled into a bad sitcom or something. It all just makes me feel worse and worse. I still can't get over this whole weird bizarre situation. How can this really be happening? I still don't think I really believe it. I can't accept this as reality, and I think this is why I can't come to a real decision about what to do, where to go and how to cope with all this.

And then the announcement comes that afternoon. Jamie comes bursting into the room clutching a piece of paper tightly. "The date is here!" He cries. Everyone looks up from whatever they're doing in shock. From this reaction, I'm positive no one else was really, deep down expecting this to happen. "It's a bit sooner than we originally thought, in 10 days time the lockdown is coming. I guess they have their reasons for it happening so quickly, maybe they've seen something, but anyway, guess what?" He looks at us expectantly for so long that a slight murmuring starts up. "We're going to announce it, on our national news segment, how great is this? Thanks everyone. Thanks Leah."

I blush as soon as my name is mentioned, not in pride or anything, but in pure unadulterated embarrassment. I'm humiliated that all this crazy stuff is happening because of me. I'm the one who originally found this 'virus' madness and somehow managed to create a mad snowball. Nothing I can do will stop it, and to be honest, I feel like I'm the only one with my head screwed on that knows the truth. None of this is real.

Questions fly about the practical arrangements, mostly about food since we won't exactly be able to pop out to the supermarket. Nice to see where everyone's priorities lie. According to the latest plans, everyone has to register where they'll be, kind of like a census, and the armed forces will bring us basic supplies, twice a week. Jamie thinks they'll also use this time to try and locate any signs of infection. Everything else has to be stocked up on beforehand. And, out of interest, the budget set aside by the prime minister, or whoever sorts that out, just about covers two weeks so there's definitely no plans for it to go on any longer than that.

Jamie goes on to tell us the plans regarding the infection. People are being urged to take themselves to hospital now, before the lockdown starts, for their own safety and that of their families. Special hotlines have been set up so people can report anyone they suspect, anyone looking unwell or acting out of character. Our news anchors will be working hard over the next few days to convince people that it is in their best interests to get every ill person to hospital or we'll never be able to get all of this under control. I quickly lose interest in Jamie's voice droning on and tune it all out.

I subconsciously find myself looking at Jake. He was the one I was trying to impress with the video in the first place, and now I'm pretty sure he can't even bring himself to look at me. Great. That's just marvellous. This is officially the stupidest thing I've done to impress a boy. And that includes the time I told Kriss Birnam that Tony Hawks was coming to 'perform skateboarding tricks' at my 13th birthday party.

Come to think of it that was the last time he spoke to me as well.

I'm so done with boys.

# TEN

So, out of simple indecision, I continue to go to work every day. It’s awful and humiliating. I don't know if it's my own paranoia and feelings about myself, but I just try and keep my head down, avoiding too much conversation and contact with anyone. I'm glad I'm facing the music though, and have actually managed to drag myself here. Not showing up to work would cause me to be the star of gossiping and bitching at the moment and I just can't bear the thought of adding any fuel to those flames. I'd never be able to come back afterwards, knowing everyone was stuck here because of me, and I didn't even have the decency to suffer through it myself. I'd have to go back to the job hunt.

At least, that's the reason I've given myself. It's the mantra I repeat over and over in my head—at home, on the way to work, and even after locking myself in the toilets when my emotions get the better of me.

If I'm totally honest, when I got home from work that first day, full of determination, I rang my mum. I told her nothing was going to keep me away from them in this difficult time and I was on the next train, screw my job. They need me and I'm the only one who can look after them.

Her response?

"Oh don't worry dear, it'll be fine. It's only a precaution and we're happy to be in for a few days, it won't really change our routine that drastically. There's bound to be loads of good TV, and we'll stock up on magazines. Plus Felix is here anyway."

I was so angry at her when I hung up. There's no way she's taking this seriously enough. Does she not realise she might never see me again?

Once I calmed down, I realised she doesn't share my paranoia for apocalypse prophecies and is just treating this virus like any other health warning. She was also right about me not throwing away what could potentially be a life changing career opportunity. I just can't help feeling a bit neglected and a bit of the old sibling-rivalry-Felix-was-always-the-favoured-child routine.

So at work I'm just concentrating and trying to cope with the *'Countdown to Lockdown'*. Our clever marketing team came up with that one and they could work for a tabloid with those kinds of word-play skills. I don't really contribute much, but that doesn't seem to matter. I'm the face of it all. As we are the most up-to-date news channel, Jamie continues to keep my photograph showing regularly. Apparently it's to give the story a human element, without showing any victims and gore. Thankfully, he let me pose for a new photo, which has replaced the hideous one used before. I even had proper make up and my hair done. I'm sure, in my normal state of mind, I'd have been terribly excited about the whole thing.

It's ironic, that all I wanted was a decent career, and to be someone important. Doesn't everyone dream of making an impact on the planet in some small way? That dream has pretty much come true, and I'm the most miserable I've ever been. I'm just waiting for it all to come back around and bite me on the arse.

As I'm not really doing a lot of work, I'm more just filling the time trying to look busy. I spend my time continually looking online, trying to find out people's reactions to all of this. I mean normal people, not nutters who have been predicting this kind of thing forever, or people whose bank balances depend on them believing it. A lot of forums are highly focused on the lockdown; arguing its usefulness, debating how long it'll take to rid the virus, discussing the ideas. Basically, the kind of questions and arguments you'd expect.

But Facebook is as usual filled with innocuous statuses about nights out and dinner plans. No one seems too concerned about this happening. No one seems to be taking it seriously. No one is even really talking about it. In fact, the odd mentions have been about how there's no way they will stay indoors and follow this rubbish. Can people really be more interested in photographs of other people's food than the threat to their freedom?

The promise of extra money has everyone here in a fantastic mood, at least. I'm sure Jamie is riding this wave of positive thinking as much as he can, knowing that the following weeks are going to be tough. I have a permanent happy expression plastered on my face, but all I can focus on is the moment this all comes crashing down around me. I'm sure I never used to be so pessimistic, but then again, I have never been in such a knife edge position before.

I don't discuss with anyone, even Michelle, about the ignorance from the general public. I think one more person thinking like me could bring the entire operation down very quickly. It seems like no one else is considering checking social media, which is crazy for a bunch of supposed news researchers, but there you go. Maybe everyone else is just enjoying the buzz, trying to prolong it for as long as possible. To keep hold of the happy futures that are just within our reach. Someone must be using Google Alerts for all the good stories about us, because now and again I hear them being yelled out. Each one has no effect on me. I must be too far gone.

Everyone is busying themselves with the presentation of today's reports on the national news segment, which will be relayed again on our usual show. It's going to be based on new science research from Mexico containing theories as to why this has happened, and been allowed to get so out of control. Sounds like more scare tactics to me. As far as I know, not one person has seen a real victim or attack, so how this is *out of control* yet is beyond me. They must have used up every resource and angle for signs to look out for over the last few days, so are trying to keep it fresh and exciting. The sad thing is, as the theories are relayed, I've already heard of all of them. Whoever this scientist is has obvious gotten every crack pot idea online, and is passing them off as real possibilities based on his own experiments. I shake my head, but continue to keep my opinions silent.

As I look at the clock, my heart sinks. There is only eight days now until the lockdown, and there has been no discouraging comments from anyone important, no signs that it's going to be called off. The arrangements seem to have all been made, everyone is happy to comply because they don't want to end up starving and alone; even the ones who are convinced it won't happen are registering, probably simply to humour the idea. All I feel like I can do now is try and hold it together, get through the next few days without having a full on mental breakdown, and just see exactly what transpires.

# ELEVEN

The next few days pass in a blur. I feel as if I have been shoved in the middle of one of those film scenes where I simply sit in my desk chair while everyone else whizzes around me, chatting excitedly and busily sorting everything out. I'm dizzy with it all. The announcements have been coming in thick and fast, always by us first, of course. From the houses of Parliament, from other countries, from leading experts. How there are leading experts in AM13, since it's only come to light recently, I'll never know.

We're all registered to the office now, so we're pretty screwed if we decide not to stay here. The warnings are being announced on television hourly: don't forget to register for food supplies, get to the hospital now if you have any health concerns, report anyone you think might have it that isn't doing it themselves, stock up on everything you think you'll need as requests cannot be put in after, always be prepared for outbursts of violent behaviour when out in public until the lockdown. It's also plastered all over billboards, newspapers, the Internet, so anyone who doesn't follow these simple instructions has no one to blame but themselves.

Despite all of the planning, the preparations, the money going into it, I just can't understand how they're going to pull it off. I can't see that they're going to keep every single healthy person in the whole of the UK locked inside their own homes. It's clear that people are already totally ignoring the health warnings. People aren't reporting every sniff and moment of tiredness like they're supposed to. Like every potential disaster, no one thinks it will happen to them. The hotlines set up for people reporting other illness are a constant stream of prank calls and people ratting out noisy neighbours and enemies, just hoping to get them in a bit of trouble.

I still seem to be the only person in this whole damn office that is trying to gauge public opinion. Ok, so it means I spend most of my days on Facebook, but it's useful. No one cares about it, not really. It's just a joke. I can see what a lot of the remarks are getting at as well. Where is the proof? All the video clips shown have been seen a hundred times, there's nothing new. And none from the UK anyway, so how do we know the virus is supposed to have reached here? They could be doing this lockdown way too early. We could all be free again, and then it hits. We also don't know a single thing about who is working on a cure, or antidote, which is surely the key to our freedom. Any information regarding this is so vague and glosses over all the vital details. I have started trying to relay this information and questions to people, but I'd have more luck talking to a brick wall.

And then it arrives. The final morning meeting, the day before it all happens.

"Ok gang, tomorrow is the day," Jamie addresses us all, happy as anything. He really is over the moon about this story; he's never referred to us all as pleasantly as 'gang' before. "Pack your bags tonight, and get here bright and early tomorrow morning. All the beds have been set up in the hall as you have seen, I know it's not ideal, but I promise you now, it will all be worth it." Pause for laughter. "According to what we know, enough stuff for a fortnight will be plenty, but just in case we have installed washing machines and plenty of facilities for your convenience."

Everyone's hand seems to rise up at the same time, and questions fire up from every direction. It all seems pointless to me. All I can think about is how unfair it is, us being forced to stay here for two weeks, under the threat of starvation. Human rights, where are you now?

Anyway, it's not going to work. No one else in this country will follow through, so I'm sure we'll be here for no longer than one night. Then we'll have to spend the next month with Jamie grumbling over the failure, and costs of having everything installed. Great, I'm sure the blame will be directed at me.

That's when I decide. I'm just going to pack my bags and play along with this little charade, and then when it inevitably all falls through I'll just walk straight out of here and insist on going home, just for a couple of days. I know my parents don't really need me there, but it just suddenly feels like the last six months since I've visited have been forever. I just want to check in on everyone, and see some friendly faces. Now that I think about her properly, hasn't mum been commenting on a lot of doctor's appointments in our conversations recently? God have I been that self-absorbed that I didn't notice her getting ill?

I let out a huge sigh as I walk through the door that evening. Then, as is my very worrying new habit, I grab a glass of wine and get on the phone. First I ring mum, and listen to her talk about herself in detail. She seems so happy to have someone to moan to about her back and chest pains. I feel so awful, usually I just go on at her about my petty issues. Then, in the spirit of making things up to people, I ring everyone I can think of, just to see how they feel about everything and have a general long overdue catch up on their lives.

It's then that I realise truly how selfish I've been, obsessed with my own life and my own needs. I've been so concerned with my so-called career and slight money issues, that I didn't even know that Rachel, my best friend from school, is pregnant and my cousin, Ethan, has been engaged for three months.

I laugh and cry through all these calls, which just reaffirms to everyone that I'm mad, as I think they've always suspected. It almost feels in a weird way like I'm saying goodbye, and I just can't figure out why. I know this is all crap, I know it’s all a hoax gone way too far, and even if the whole lockdown thing comes into place, which I'm sure it won't, we'll all be back be to normal in at the absolutely most, a month.

Except deep, deep down, in the place where I hide all my secrets and problems I don't want to face, I know that's not what I believe at all. The hollow feeling in my chest tells me that I kind of think that tomorrow everything is going to change. Maybe it's just that everything is going to change for me. Maybe I just know that after this nightmare, people will not be so keen to talk to me anymore.

Yeah, that must be it. It's not exactly like I truly believe that AM13 is real, and a zombie apocalypse is heading our way. Because that would make me a crazy person. Wouldn't it?

Starting to feel a little bit drunk, I notice the wine bottle is empty. Unfortunately there's no one else here for me to blame, so I must have drunk more than I thought. I realise I still need to pack a few things into a suitcase. As I'm trying to convince myself that I won't be staying long I don't even think about what I'm chucking into my bag, just a few clothes and a couple of books. It's not like I really care about what I'll look like, I don't really feel the need to impress anyone at the office any more since I've completely given up on Jake. Wow I must be more upset than I thought.

As I lie in bed, just starting to drift off to sleep, I jump up bolt right. Hair straighteners. How could I be so stupid as to forget to pack them? When my heart stops racing I remember, I don't care what I've packed, it's all irrelevant anyway. So I try to settle back down, but suddenly I'm not as comfortable, or as tired.

I know exactly what's bothering me, but I'm not going to give in. I'm not going to be there for long so I really don't need to worry.

But after 15 minutes of tossing and turning, I surrender. Maybe this whole casual attitude towards packing is stupid. I get out of bed and empty my suitcase and start again, beginning with those damn hair straighteners.

# TWELVE

I huff as I toss my case onto my new temporary, tiny bed. Despite the fact I've already decided that I'm not staying for very long, I still feel disheartened. I can just imagine how pissed off everyone else is about having to live in such cramped conditions with absolutely no real privacy for a fortnight, or however long were going to be here. I know we all go out for drinks occasionally after work, but are we really friends? I already know the answer to this, most friendships between colleagues is circumstantial.

I can predict a lot of tension breaking out, working together on such an intense project, and then having no escape at the end of the day. I just know Jamie will be really strict here. He totally believes in all of this, and then of course, we can set a precedent for everyone else. This just sucks.

As I wander out into the corridor, I spot Jake. Wow he's looking really ill now, kind of pale and sweaty. I chuckle to myself thinking I'm surprised he hasn't been forced to the hospital particularly by Jamie. He looks exactly the way a real life zombie should look.

I walk over to him and try to talk, but he could not make it clearer that he doesn't want to say anything to me. I can't believe he's acting like this. It must be because he thinks this is all my fault. Well that's just stupid. It's not exactly like I love being here bloody locked up like some sort of caged animal. I didn't mean for any of this to happen. I wish I'd never sent that idiotic link in the first place, then none of this would be happening.

Work that day is actually not that much different to normal, which shocks me. I still don't really do anything useful, not that anyone notices. Also, no one really seems to be commenting too much about having to stay here. Not in front of my face anyway, maybe behind my back so they can throw in some choice words about me while they're at it. Everyone seems quite accepting.

Well, except me of course, who just can't even begin to take it in stride. What is wrong with me?

Oh God, that's a can of worms I don't want to open. I seem to be spending more and more time asking myself that question which is worrying. Although I guess I do have a good excuse.

At lunch time, I casually glance out of the window onto the street below, and there are loads of people still walking around, as if this isn't even happening.

"Typical," I mutter under my breath. Oops, I must have said it louder than I thought because everyone turns to stare at me. "Look," I clarify. "I just knew we'd end up being the only ones following this lockdown. It was so obvious no one else cares enough to take it seriously. That woman even has her pram and toddler. She's not too worried about infection if she's got small children out with her."

This leads to much debate and confusion over the vague information given out. Of course, I could have warned them of that if anyone had listened. It seems the lockdown is not going to be officially enforced until tonight. People are probably stocking up, no one is really sure about what will happen with the food deliveries is the main argument given.

Fine. If they want to delude themselves, I'll just leave them to it.

That argument really highlighted the main issues as far as I'm concerned. It all happened far too quickly, with too many plan changes and not enough information. I may have not paid full attention to it all, but obviously I wasn't the only one. In all the panic, no one has been given enough clear details. There might have been hourly updates from doctors, politicians, etc. But so much has been forgotten, or ignored. For instance, who exactly is going to enforce this rule and get everyone indoors? Police? Isn't that going to put them in a difficult position if they're out free, telling others to go in, lock their doors and don't come back out again until they're given explicit permission? There have been too many mistakes in the past, when it comes to health scares, so people aren't going to feel sufficiently at risk to be told what to do. Especially with something that I think is really extreme. It seems they have gone straight to the final protocol, rather than taking all the small steps first.

Suddenly I'm full of rage. This is just idiotic. I storm into Jamie's office and rant for about 10 minutes about everything I think has been dealt with incorrectly with this virus situation. When I stop, panting, unable to catch my breath, he answers me

"The information has been sketchy in places I agree, but we're constantly being given different things to tell the public. We're only relaying the plans, not making them. It has been hard and no, I don't know how they're going to follow through with this, I don't think anybody really does, they have put it into place too quickly and without thinking it through thoroughly, but we'll just have to see what happens. I can't tell you why it has moved so drastically, so fast, because I don't know. Obviously there are reasons behind it that we aren't being told. In my opinion if this does work, it will save many, many lives."

I roll my eyes, I just can't even start to tolerate Jamie's weird belief in zombies today, so I just turn and walk out without saying another word.

...

All afternoon, and into the evening, I find myself wandering over to the windows, watching all the people out on the street, laughing and messing around, totally uncaring. Everyone else is either still working or are in the hall arguing over what to watch on the television. Michelle eventually joins me with a cigarette in hand.

"Don't worry." She smiles at my shocked face. "If we

aren't allowed outside they can hardly keep up the smoking ban." When this fails to get a laugh out of me, she changes the subject to what she knows I really want to talk about. "I'm not staying either, you know."' I whip round immediately, stunned. "I know you want to go, I can see it. When you leave I'm coming with you. I'm not staying here with all these losers. It'll be no fun."

The look on my face lets her know I don't exactly think it's fun now. That's when she produces a bottle of vodka she has hidden in her bag, which has the ability to totally change my opinion. Funny how alcohol can have that effect. We decide to sneak down into the small garden area outside work. Technically we aren't breaking any rules; we'll still be within the walls. Jamie might not look too kindly on it but right now, I really couldn't care less.

We spend the rest of the night getting progressively tipsier on screwdrivers, which seem to get stronger as the night wears on. This means we don't feel the cold so much, so we spend the time planning our epic escape from the clutches of work. We're talking about all the things we'll do when we've gained our freedom, which get more extreme and ridiculous the drunker we get. As if we've been locked up for years and years.

I know I'm going to regret the alcohol tomorrow, but tonight it's such a nice relief to laugh, and joke, and forget about all the crap that's going on, with the one person who I know I can trust to not blame me or hold any of this against me in the future. I love Michelle.

# THIRTEEN

The next day is awful. If I wasn't already here, I'd definitely phone in sick. The headache and nausea is unbearable. To make it worse, Jamie is more determined than ever that we are going to make sure the lockdown is followed through. We are the voice of reason. What a delightful responsibility. As far as I can tell, this has been the biggest failure ever. I can still see people walking around outside as if nothing is happening. Obviously the police crackdown failed. Shocker.

The enthusiasm from before is not evident today. Everyone is sitting, sipping hot drinks, looking as if they wish this day was over, and it hasn't even begun yet. No one looks as pristine as usual. Suits and smart clothing are nowhere to be seen, just sweatpants and hoodies. Some girls haven't even bothered with makeup which actually gives this whole thing a teenage-sleepover feel. Someone just needs to get out some popcorn and put on a horror film. Which is ironic, considering were trying to convince the world we're living in one.

I don't think me and Michelle are the only ones with a hangover. Most people look a little green. Last night, the 'prison quarters' did sound quite noisy from outside.

The only person who does not look like his bad mood and ill feeling has come from a late night of drinking and fun, is Jake. He looks truly terrible.

...

After the morning meeting, which actually turned into more of a collective moan once Jamie had gone, we all shuffle off to our desks. I instantly log onto Facebook. I can’t help it, it's become reflex, and I'm actually shocked by what I see. Of course, there is the typical complaints that I half-expected: people sent home by the police, people who received the meals on wheels type service moaning about the food and just general little niggles about how this is actually happening.

But that is not the shocking part. A few people, people I know and I'm positive are actually sane, are urging others to do what we're supposed to and get indoors. New video links, newspaper articles and photo proof that I haven't seen before attached to their statuses. Statuses filled with frightened convincing arguments. Wow, fear mongering truly works, who knew. Where the hell have these new attitudes come from? Has something happened in the outside world we don't know about?

After a stunned pause, I log onto all the national newspapers websites to see what they have to say. Maybe I'll find the answer there. It is immediately obvious that these people are still at work, I wonder if they have to live in their office, trapped like us. The front pages are all along the lines of 'Biggest Disaster in UK History'. Well I can't exactly argue with that.

The more in-depth articles are all trying to work out exactly what the plan was and how it was supposed to work. All the questions I expected are being asked. How much of the taxpayers money has gone into this initiative? What was this was supposed to achieve? Where is the evidence that this virus is such a threat to us that we have to be locked up? I feel really nervous reading all this because I know this is just the beginning. It won't be long until it somehow comes back to me. I'll probably become the most hated woman in Britain, and I'll have to change my identity and move.

Suddenly, I look up and notice the office is all abuzz. Everyone is crowded round a computer talking excitedly. I walk over there to find out that Aaron, one of the tech guys, has been sent some information about an AM13 incident that happened in the early hours of the morning, in England. At Heathrow airport. I had already seen this video earlier today on Twitter, so it's no surprise to me. What I can't understand is why they're all taken in by it? An English strain to the hoax was obviously going to happen. All it shows is some idiot messing around pretending to lurch at people threateningly. It's purposely shot on a really shaky mobile phone so you can't even really see anything. Granted the screaming is realistic, but as it's supposed to be happening at some ridiculous hour in the morning, it would be easy to get the few people in the terminal involved. I roll my eyes and leave the room.

When I come back in, they've got Jamie watching the video and he has gone really pale. It takes all I've got not to laugh out loud. Then he speaks solemnly.

"Guys, this follows the daily report I've had from the hospital exactly. They've got a guy of this description in quarantine, along with, what I assume are the other people from the video. Two of them have got massive skin injuries that look like bite marks, but no one is really sure of anything exact as the victims aren't coherent. The police have said we can't report this yet as there's no real information. But this, it proves everything." He stands up to emphasise his point. People are nodding and murmuring agreements.

I, however, could not disagree more; it doesn't prove a single thing. If it's even true, it's just coincidence. Something like this happened in America a while back, people were taking drugs that made them bite other people. If this had happened at any other time no one would be paying it any attention.

Now though, it has got everyone really excited. The enthusiasm is instantly back and better than ever. I think this makes my colleagues all feel like we're following through on the lockdown for a valid reason. We're not all going to end up a joke and we are actually going to save everyone's lives. People are starting to feel that they're in the right place. It's safe here.

They're all idiots.

I give up trying to look like I'm doing anything useful and watch the people milling about outside, but I do notice it's less than yesterday. As the darkness starts to set in, there's hardly anyone to be seen. Even if that story about Heathrow is not allowed to be reported on the news yet, everyone is still seeing it, especially since it's leaked online. They must be crazy to think it's been kept secret.

Michelle and I end up outside again in the late evening. She's the only person I really want to be around from here, everyone else is just driving me nuts. Tonight we don't just sit in one place, sort of hidden. We wander round trying to get glimpses of the streets around us. We really get the giggles when we see some houses that have boarded up their windows. What are they trying to stop from coming in? If this whole situation wasn't so tragic—and my fault—I'd be spending a lot more time laughing at how quickly this madness has escalated.

...

I barely sleep at all that night. My brain just can't shut off. I'm driving myself to madness with all of this worrying. It's not doing me any good, or getting me anywhere at all. So when the early morning comes I get up, full of determination that I'm just going to take each day, each minute if needs be, as it comes.

Of course, a revelation like that needs caffeine, so I plod over to the next room where the coffee machine is to make myself one, trying to decide how to be positive today, and what I'm going to do to make myself feel a bit better.

As I glance out of the window, something stops my

trail of thought. There's a lone woman outside, who is all dishevelled and in a bad way. Her trousers have been practically ripped off her body, revealing a big gash on her leg. Something awful has happened to her. The possibilities race through my mind. She looks crazy, comatose, like she's sleepwalking or something. The loss of blood from her injury must have sent her into a state of delirium. I bang on the window to let her know I'm there and cry out for someone to call an ambulance. I grab the kitchen roll and turn.

As I'm about to rush out the room, a feeling of unease spreads over me and stops me dead. I glance back out onto the road where she's stood and a cold chill comes over me. Now she's looking this way and I can see her face fully. Her jaw has disconnected and is hanging down from her face and in her hand is a severed human arm.

# FOURTEEN

The next thing I'm aware of is ice cold water hitting my face, making me jump up with a start. When did I fall asleep? I start to try and voice what I saw, but my panicky garbled voice is not making any sense to anyone. I jump up onto my feet and point out the window gesturing wildly as I can't quite find the words to explain the horror. Not one person is showing any signs of recognition or understanding of what I'm saying, which just causes me to freak out more. The tears are burning my skin and my throat is starting to feel constricted. I give up trying to form words, and concentrate on breathing properly again.

When I actually calm down enough to think to look out the window, there's no one there. The battered woman has gone. Did I imagine her? Have I started hallucinating? Is that what all this worry has done to me? Oh God, now I have to try and pretend to the others that I'm sane so they don't instantly send me to some psych ward.

I sit down quietly, hoping that everyone will simply assume my ranting was due to me passing out. That's a side effect, right? I'm starting to actually see faces in front of my eyes, rather than just the messy blur of before.

"Sorry," Michelle mutters, almost to herself. "I didn't think that the water would shock you that much, I just, didn't know what else to do. You were yelling for an ambulance. I ran in and found you on the floor, and you were out for so long."

On the outside, I look cool and calm, but my brain is whirring round and round trying to decide if what I saw was real, and if so how to explain it. I'm aware of the concerned chatter surrounding me, about how to 'deal' with me, but I'm not affected by it. Suddenly a loud shouting that seems to come from nowhere breaks through my thought barrier. Is it her? Am I about to be proven sane? Everyone dashes to the window to see what is happening and there, lying in the road is a man who has fallen off his motorbike. He looks pretty messed up, so on instinct we all run outside, prison sentence forgotten. I can hear someone on the phone to the emergency services as we go. All thoughts about me and my little incident have been immediately forgotten.

The cool refreshing air hits my face and takes my breath away. I pause to regain myself, by which time everyone else has already reached the gate. They're shaking it and screaming for it to be opened. No one has their pass with them, I guess they're all tucked away in their bags, I know mine is. We've had no use for them.

It's the only way to get in and out the gate, for data protection purposes apparently. Security must have another method though, and I'm sure they can hear everyone, they aren't exactly being quiet. I turn desperately to look in the window and see one of the security guards, Lucas, looking at us all, but doing nothing. As I try and communicate with him that he needs to open the bloody gate now—after all it is a matter of life and death—he turns away. What the hell? Surely he can't put the lockdown before this.

"The medics are on their way!" I hear one voice above the rest, which makes me feel slightly more at ease.

When I finally get a good look at the injured man, I realise, in his eyes, he looks utterly panicked and I really can't work out why. Surely as a biker, he has had minor accidents before. He doesn't look as bad as I first assumed, it's mostly surface wounds and he's a big tough guy so I'm certain he will be fine. I suddenly realise he has been staring in the same direction the entire time. The fainting must have muddled my brain because it's taken me forever to suss out that something is not right.

He isn't looking at us; he hasn't even glanced our way. That's really weird considering all the noise we're making. My colleagues are all shouting out words of support and encouragement to him and he's completely ignoring them. What he's looking at must be either more interesting than a bunch of people yelling at him, or absolutely terrifying. If I could find out what it was, I could decide on my next move and hopefully help him.

I'll never get any closer to the gate because everyone else is shoving and pushing there, plus I might not be able to see anyway, so I run further along the wall.

A loud crash causes me to spin back round to face the others. Someone has climbed over the gate. How the hell have they managed that? It's huge. It was probably one of the guys trying to act like some kind of caring action hero, hoping to get themselves laid while were stuck here. The sad thing is I imagine it'll work and he will have all the girls fawning over him later. I rush back to see which idiot it was, and it's Tom, one of the HR guys.

He gets over to the motorcyclist quickly and tries to talk him round and keep him calm. He's actually quite good at this. I begrudgingly think I may have been too quick to assume he has selfish intentions. The guy doesn't look at Tom, not once. He keeps his eyes fixated where they were before. After a while, Tom catches on to this and follows his gaze. I have never seen a man go from pure adrenalin rush high to pale terrified shock so quickly. Ok, what the hell is going on?

Tom races back over to the gate, abandoning the injured man and his chance to be a hero. The look in his eyes jolts shock and more panic through my system. I instantly know exactly what he has seen. "Get back. Move away from the gate!" I scream at everyone. The fear in my voice must be obvious, because everyone jumps back as if they have been electrocuted. That doesn't stop me. "Move, come on!" I'm pulling people backwards, throwing them to the ground. I can't think about anything except my goal of clearing the way and keeping everyone else away from harm.

Tom jumps and tries to pull himself up, as I guess he did before, but the fear must have got to him and the pressure has made his palms too sweaty because he keeps slipping back down. I've been so focused on getting everyone out of his way, that there's no one left to help him, to try and push him up and get him over the top quicker.

Then we all see the horror descending on us. It happens in slow motion, and I can't even begin to move a muscle to do anything useful. The woman I saw earlier, the monstrous, bloody, destroyed woman is back. This time, however, she isn't alone. She's ambling over with two men, if you can call them that, both in a similar condition to her. She heads straight for the easy target, the biker trapped by his own injuries, whereas the others drag Tom, kicking and screaming to the ground. And, there's no other way to describe this...

They start eating them.

# FIFTEEN

This is my fault. A man, well two men are dead because of me. I may as well have murdered them myself. If I had just said something to someone about seeing that awful woman from up in the office, or shouted sooner, or mentioned to someone that the biker was staring at something up the street. *Something.* If I hadn't been so bloody obsessed with pulling everyone out of harm's way, we could have pulled Tom over the gate.

He would still be alive and here now. I assume that the biker had already been attacked, and that's what had caused him to crash. His injuries kind of suggest that much, so I feel much worse about Tom. Plus I kind of actually knew him, which always makes a death hit you harder. I mean, we worked in the same office for months. It's not like we particularly talked to each other much more than saying hello, but still.

And now, I've contributed towards his death. I'll always be a part of his history. In the worst possible way. I did not know it was possible to hate myself this much.

I'm perfectly aware that no one would have believed me. How could they, when I didn't believe what I'd seen myself? But then, at least I would have tried. At least I would have done something. Then I wouldn't feel so God damn awful. I look around at everyone else's faces. They all look as stunned and disbelieving as I feel. I'm sure that my expression is mirrored in all of theirs, just tainted with the knowledge that I actually had the power to prevent all of this from happening.

As soon as the horror plummeted into a feeding frenzy outside, before any of us even had a split second to react, the emergency services arrived. The paramedics rushed out in blood-splattered white protective boiler suits, armed with all sorts of medical equipment. They injected the infected in the back of the head, while they were feeding and distracted. This caused them to flop to the ground, motionless. They then went on to sedate the victims in a similar way and bundled them all into the back of the ambulance.

We all just stood there, silent and unmoving, while they drove away without even acknowledging our existence. It felt like hours before someone finally turned around and went back inside. We all followed slowly, like sheep, and no one has uttered a word since.

Jamie stands up and clears his throat as if he's preparing to say something, but falls into silence. Finally he opens his mouth again, and this time manages to speak. "Well, what can I say? This comes as a massive shock. For an attack to happen on our own doorstep. To one of our own men." No one has even lifted their heads to look at him properly "Tom was great. Such a hard worker and I know a brilliant friend too many of you. For him to die in such an unjust fashion is just heart wrenching." Murmurs of agreement show Jamie he has finally got everyone's attention "But his death won't be in vain. We have just witnessed the threat of AM13 with our own eyes, and now we have to work hard to ensure every single person puts themselves into quarantine. That this doesn't happen to anyone else."

Jamie's speech puts a real fire in my belly. He's right. Of course he is. I can't do anything to save Tom now, but I can stop anyone else from getting hurt. We are in the unique position of having a voice that the whole of the country can hear. It's only now I appreciate how hard it must have been for people to get videos of the attacks. No one here even thought about it. But how else do you prove what you've seen?

As soon as I get a chance, I ring my mother. I try and tell her what's happened today, but obviously under all the stress and upset I sound more like I'm cracking up than anything else. I can tell she's only half listening, so I take my chance and speak to Felix. He might be a typical stubborn 17-year-old, but he's also the only person who might take me seriously. I stumble through all the events of the day and beg him to get mum and dad indoors permanently. He laughs and says he will do his best, and I breathe a sigh of relief. I know he'll do it. He may be so laid back he's practically horizontal, but I know I can trust him. We promise faithfully to text each other all the time with updates.

I then decide to get online, and tell everyone what I've seen. I target all the social media sites, where people have been the most critical of the lockdown. I find myself writing over and over again that the quarantine is the answer, and by getting indoors, people will be giving themselves a real chance at survival. I just hope people listen.

Michelle wanders out of the hall and over to my desk. She sits in silence while I continue to type manically, and it's not until I get a good look at her that I realise she has been crying. I can tell by her puffy eyes. She's just sitting in the chair and I'm at a loss of what to say. Nothing I can say or do will make her feel better, so I just pull her in for a hug.

After about five minutes, she finally speaks. "I can't believe what happened. I don't think I believed it, not really. I tried to. I pretended to." she trails off. I nod, still not knowing what to say. "We are never in a million years only going to be locked up for two weeks. They'll never get rid of the virus that quickly. How do they intend to do that? Shut down all international flights? They didn't even think to do that leading up to the lockdown, which might be the exact reason it came here. The first video we saw in England was at Heathrow after all." She looks up at me, desperation evident in her eyes. "We're going to die here. Do you realise that? There's no other possible outcome. How are they going to get all the infected people cured? I don't think they even have a cure. In fact, I don't think they even know what's caused it. If you think about it, nothing has been confirmed. I just. I don't want to die here, not at work for Christ's sake! Surrounded by people I don't really even care for."

...

As I lie in bed that night, sleep totally evades me again. These sleepless nights are surely going to catch up with me soon. I can't stop thinking about Michelle. I've never seen her like that. She only has one mode: happy and bubbly. After her rant, we talked for hours, about people from her past that she'd like to see again, old boyfriends, college friends she'd lost touch with, family members. I could still see the fear etched in her face, and the knowledge that she won't ever see them again.

The worst part about it is she voiced everything I'd been too scared to really think about. In a hypothetical way yes, I've thought about it nonstop, but only in an 'it'll never happen' way, not for real. Not like this.

How could we leave this place though? After what we saw today. For all its faults—the main thing being it's our workplace—it's safe. We'd be insane to leave. We're protected here. We're registered here. How would we even begin to survive out there, with those horrible flesh-munching creatures?

# SIXTEEN

I'm up hours before everyone else again and way before the morning meeting. I decide not to waste any more time procrastinating and to actually do something useful. Not work, of course. I'm beyond the stage of thinking that's going to help me. I search through all the online forums and websites, dedicated to AM13 and similar viruses. I've already read everything before, but now I'm looking at it through new eyes. Not with the sceptical attitude from before, but as someone who has seen the threat first hand.

I make notes of everything and anything that could be of any use to me, in any small way possible. The survival techniques are actually fantastic, things you'd never normally think about. The bug out bag tips are incredibly useful. In fact, I'm determined that if I do end up leaving here, which I fully intend to do at some point, the items listed will definitely be coming with me.

I'm just starting to feel a bit more positive about my ability to cope with this situation, when I come across the section detailing what to do if you cross someone infected, particularly if you get bitten. It's just so morbid. There's no other way to describe it. It states that, once the early signs of AM13 have been detected, it's already too late. Your organs will end up shutting down, causing pain and hallucinations and finally you'll reach the comatose stage commonly called being a 'zombie'. The only way to stop an infected person is to kill them, and not just any death will do—the brain has to be completely destroyed.

I feel sick to my stomach at the thought of having to kill anyone. I can't even consider the prospect of it happening to me—even infected people trying to eat me, like those ones who ended Tom's life. Murder is a horrific crime, there must be another way. When they find a cure, won't all the people who followed these rules be arrested? Ending someone's life is a criminal act, whatever the situation, surely? Even if it *is* self-defence. I just, I know I won't be able to do it. Will I actually be able to survive this outbreak outside of these walls? Hopefully the situation outside won't be too dire. If everyone else follows the lockdown well, there shouldn't be too many of those things out there. This is terrifying, we could die. Then again, if Michelle is right, we'll end up dying here anyway, and then I'll always wonder what if?

Michelle is still in a morose mood today, so I take her quietly to one side, and tell her what I have been researching and planning. She's unsurprisingly completely shocked that I'm really considering this. I can tell she thought I just took her sombre rants yesterday as temporary insanity. Some kind of cabin fever. She halfheartedly argues with me that there's no way we can do this. Even if we can survive infection and starvation, we'll never be able to evade the authorities, who are supposed to be really cracking down on people ignoring the lockdown now, but I can tell deep down she's all for it. She's always loved adventures and it doesn't get more exciting than this.

By the time the morning meeting comes round, I feel like I've already been awake for hours. Jamie's expression is very serious, so I know whatever he's going to tell us won't be good. When he speaks though, it’s worse than I could have ever imagined. Tonight, on our national news segment, we'll put out the message that anyone seen out on the streets after midnight tonight, will be considered infected and therefore a threat. They will be taken to hospital instantly, and any signs of resistance will force an arrest. All the police will also be issued with guns, so if things get serious, you risk being killed. The real crackdown is just beginning.

I feel hot and panicky as I consider the implications of this. Escape is definitely not an option now. What the hell are we going to do? I glance at Michelle and her face looks just as frightened and pissed off as I feel. While everyone else shoots off questions, trying to work out why this has suddenly got so serious, my mind is working overtime, thinking about what Jamie has said and any possible solutions for us. Then it hits me.

I suddenly understand what really happened yesterday. What I had originally mistaken for a sedative injection from health professionals was actually a brutal murder by the authorities. They hit Tom and the others in the brain with whatever was in their hands, just like the forums said to. I think my eyes allowed me to see what they wanted to, to prevent me from breaking down more than I already did. I know this was probably the only real solution but, oh my God, poor Tom.

The thought of Tom has me rushing to the bathroom to vomit. Poor, poor Tom. They didn't even give him a chance; he might not have even been infected. A small part of me is saying to grow up. There's no way anyone could survive the injuries he sustained. And anyway, once the infection is even slightly in your blood stream, you've got no hope. But I'm blocking that part out. Rage is burning in my heart, and blood is pulsing in my ears so all I can't focus on anything rational.

I storm into the news room, and just start yelling to anyone who will listen. Everyone turns to stare at me like I've lost my mind, which I know isn't far from the truth. I'm screaming that Tom could have been saved, that we should have done something. We all just stood there like idiots and let them kill him and take him away. I'm trying to get across that murdering people, without even thinking of the consequences is not going to get us anywhere. The virus isn't going to just go away over night by bumping a few infected off, but I'm not sure it's coming across well.

After about 10 minutes I peter out, breaths coming in short and heavy. I've just run out of things to shout. I know my rage is misguided. Really, there's nothing we could do for Tom, what I'm really mad about is the fact that AM13 is real, and it's taking lives and causing infected people to maim and kill others. It's just insane. It's like a nightmare I can't wake up from.

No one says anything to me. No one is even looking at me. Oh God, I've slowly become that crazy, deluded weirdo no one wants to talk to. I look around the room, trying to catch anyone's eye. I just want someone to say something. Even if they tell me I'm wrong. Then finally, I get someone's attention. Jake. He's looking at me with such a caring expression of sympathy and understanding, I almost melt. I give him a weak smile and mouth "sorry". He starts trying to silently communicate something back to me, but I'm no longer focusing on his face. I'm noticing his greying skin, the bags under his eyes, his sweaty forehead and red bloodshot eyes.

My previous suspicions were right, he's ill. But he's definitely not normal ill. He's infected. He's actually sat here in front of me, showing signs of AM13. I can't believe I didn't realise it before. I joked about it to myself, but I guess that was back when I still didn't think the virus was real. Oh God, the panic wells up. Were locked inside, with someone who is about to become one of those beasts.

# SEVENTEEN

For a whole second, I'm totally frozen. I have no idea what I'm supposed to do. Do I scream and panic? Secretly phone the emergency services? Calmly call a meeting and tell everyone else that he's about to turn into one of those things? I think Jake senses the pure fright in my eyes, because I see a range of emotions cross his face: fear, denial, anger and then a strange kind of relief. He must want someone else to know what's going on. It must be a huge burden to tolerate on your own. Maybe he wants to be ousted so he can be cured. Well that's what he thinks will happen. I know better. When they take him away, that's the last we'll ever see of him.

I stomp across the room and pull him out by his sleeve. My ears are buzzing with the knowledge of what Jake could potentially unleash on us all. Once I'm certain were alone, I start.

"How the hell could you? Knowing you've got that—" I mouth AM13 to him, still careful, I really don't want this conversation to be overheard, "and you stay here endangering us all." I'm getting more and more worked up.

"No, no, no." he interrupts waving his hands in front of my face. "It's not what you think." I stop and look at him, perplexed. I can't tell from his expression where he's going with this. "I'm not sick, not really. It's stress. And no sleep, it always has this effect on me." I shake my head; of course he'd say that. He's scared. "It's hard to explain." he continues. He lets out a huge sigh before carrying on, which I'm sure is him just buying some time while he prepares his lie.

After he finishes talking, I'm positive that every word that comes out of his mouth is truth. His story makes me so sad. He has a son, Harry. He never told anyone here about him before, because he didn't want to be judged for his situation. Harry was conceived during a one night stand, when Jake was only 17. He tried to make a relationship work with Harry's mother, Pippa, but they were both far too young for that kind of commitment. Harry now lives with Pippa roughly 20 miles away, and because of bitter rows in the past, Jake only gets to see him one weekend every month. He says this is why he never really made much effort to get close to me, despite wanting to. He thought all of this would have put me off.

It was just coming up to Jake's weekend with Harry, when the lockdown notion started being broadcast. Pippa wouldn't hear of Harry coming up, even for a day. Just in case he couldn't make it back. Jake got so angry at her reaction, so the rows escalated, but this soon turned to heartbreak when he learned how real the virus was. Ever since the incident with Tom, he has been trying to contact Pippa, through the phone, emails, Facebook, but no success. He has no idea where they are, or even if his son is still alive.

Ok, I'm starting to see why he might be looking the way he is.

I know he could be trying to fool me with this story about a child no one has heard of before, but he says it with such a conviction that not a shadow of a doubt crosses my mind. Plus, men tend not to cry, unless it's for a genuine reason. My heart is racing with the injustice of his situation, and the fear he must be feeling. God, if I thought *I* had reason to worry.

"I'm a genius!" I suddenly cry out. I can see him looking at me strangely, so I begin to explain my plan with Michelle. I invite him to come with us on our break out mission. That way he can get to Pippas' house, and find out for certain about his son. Why didn't I think of inviting him before? With him on our side, I just know we can make it. He smiles at me sadly, and replies that he would love to come, he's thought about breaking out himself, so doing it with company would be excellent, but he just can't see it being possible.

When I press him for a further explanation he continues. "Do you really think Jamie will let us leave? They've got loads of security here. I know they think it's for our own good, to keep us safe, but its better guarded than prison. Plus, you heard the announcement this morning. If they find us, they'll kill us, and to top it off, we have no survival equipment, or access to any."

...

I go to bed that night feeling utterly downhearted. Jake's right, of course he is. If what we saw yesterday is any indication of what the outside is like, why the hell would we want to go out there and face that? Unequipped and unprepared at that? We'd have to be fucking crazy. We'd die, there's no way we'd make it. We really should just ride the lockdown out here, where we know for a fact we're safe, warm and fed. Then when it's all over, we can go and see our families or whatever. That's the sensible solution, and I know that's what we should do. I go to sleep resolved that I'm going to stay here, and just make the best of a bad situation.

But when the sun streams through my window, waking me up, I know. I just can't. The reason is simple. I don't think the lockdown will resolve anything. I can just see us being stuck inside for months, and the virus still being a threat. We are supposed to be the news station with the most up-to-date information on this exact subject, and even we don't know how they're really going to get rid of AM13. That can only mean one thing. No one knows. They have no idea, and a fortnight isn't going to change that.

My instincts are telling me that if I don't do this, if I don't at least try, I'll never see my family again. That morbid thought is terrifying, and enough to make me positive, that I can't follow the sensible road, staying shacked up here, just waiting to die. If others want to join me, well, we're all adults. They know the risks and what they will be getting themselves into. They'll have to decide for themselves if the reason they want to leave is worth the high risk of death. I know mine is. Ok, I may not have always been as close to my family as I would have liked, but I love them. And if I make it, I'll be getting a second chance.

As soon as I get an opportunity, I tell Michelle and Jake in hushed tones, that I'm going. I'm aware of everything that could go wrong and that hasn't changed my mind. Michelle is right behind me. She hasn't given me a solid reason why, her true purpose for wanting to leave, but I can tell in her eyes that there's something. That's enough for me. I don't even need Jake to respond, to know that he'll come. The idea must have been running through his mind all night, like it has mine, and to be fair, he has the most valid reason of all. Nothing will stop him from finding out what has happened to his son.

Now that were all set on our decision, we have a much worse problem to overcome. How the hell are we going to get out undetected? We know Jamie is determined we are going to stay. He doesn't want any of us meeting the same fate as Tom. I completely respect and agree with the premise of this, but it is a massive hindrance to our escape plans. This is going to take some serious thought.

Actually we have more to consider than just our getting out requirement. We need the right amount of food and supplies to survive our trip, which means we need to work out how long we'll be on the road, and if we’re going to keep out of sight to avoid being caught—by the infected and the authorities. We need to get our route exactly right. Considering we're all going to different destinations, this might be a lot more difficult than first suspected.

I try to keep it together during the work day. Try to act completely innocuous so none of my other colleagues suspect. We've considered asking others, but couldn't think of anyone else that needs to leave, or would be a good asset to our team. To be honest, the less people that know about what we're doing, the less chance of our cover being blown. I'm making a constant stream of notes and questions to consider, knowing that I will discuss it in detail with Michelle and Jake tonight.

# EIGHTEEN

That evening, we congregate outside again. Luckily, no one else has bothered to. They're all quite happy camped out in the hall. I wonder if they're gossiping about us never joining them, but then quickly realise that it hardly matters.

The parts of the town we can see from where we are, aren't looking great, to put it mildly. More windows are boarded up now and litter covers the streets. We can't see a single person now, healthy or infected. I'm not quite sure what to make of that so I just try and focus on the task at hand. Luckily, it turns out we've all spent the day secretly formulating plans, and finding possible issues, so we combine our notes.

It appears we'll actually spend a lot of our journey going the same way, which means we can stick together. This is great, because when it comes to the horrors outside, I think 'safety in numbers' will become our motto. Jake and I have the furthest to go, and we'll have to split up about three quarters of the way in the journey.

He reckons, in total the trip should only take approximately five days, with Michelle alongside us for three of them, and me only having to spend about half a day alone. He did offer to travel my last part with me, but I turned him down instantly. I know how desperate he must be to get to Harry. Plus, come on, I can last a few hours by myself. This trip is going to be so short; I can't really see anything going wrong.

We decide to start hoarding food, water, and other necessary supplies—it turns out my notes about the bug out bag will come in handy after all—at every opportunity and as discreetly as possible. We have had more than enough delivered to us anyway. No one will notice the odd thing going missing. We need to get everything we need to keep warm, fed and in relatively good health, without arousing suspicion.

I have also looked at online blogs and notes from other people, who have survived some of the outbreak out on the road. Abandoned shops are a good place to borrow from if we run out of anything, or to get weapons to defend ourselves, if it comes down to it. I guess money really counts for nothing in these sorts of situations. I can always repay anyone who I steal from afterwards anyway, or I'll make notes of the shop names and send them an online bank transfer. Then I'll have nothing to feel guilty for.

We have decided that the only way to get out of the office is quickly and at night. Maybe not the best plan in the world, but I can't see anything else working. As soon as we're ready, we're just going to make a break for it and hop over the wall. Jake thinks he knows a section that might not be covered by the security cameras. It's a risk; I can't see anyone coming after us when they realise were gone, but they might report us to the authorities. The last thing we need is them on extra alert for our faces.

The only real disagreement we have is what to do when we're out. I think we should get as far away from the office as possible, cover as many miles as we can. Jake thinks we should just hunker down in the first suitable place we find. They'll be expecting us to run and will be looking for us further away. Michelle, typically, thinks we should just play it by ear. Even though, I can't stand her casual attitude to it, I know that's what we'll end up doing.

...

The next few days seem to drag on, Jake gathering everything he can, Michelle researching and me simply paranoid that everyone else is suspicious. I can't relax for one second. I'm convinced everyone knows exactly what we're up to. Despite this, come Friday, we are actually ready to go. Excitement frizzes as I go over everything again and again in my mind. We have managed to acquire food, water, washing equipment—just in case an opportunity arises—torches, matches, bandages and a set of clean clothes. I know changing into fresh undies isn't exactly going to be my top priority—that'll be not dying—but I'm keeping optimistic that I'll get a chance. I've repacked my bag a hundred times, trying to include everything I need, without it being too heavy. We don't have anything to defend ourselves with yet, if it comes to it, which I'm almost positive it won't, but Jake knows of a building site nearby which might have some kind of useful tools. Not the best solution, but again, it'll have to do.

Michelle, Jake and I head outside for a few hours, the same as we have every other night, but this time everything is different. We are all massively on edge and can't bring ourselves to talk as much as usual. All I can focus on is how derelict everything looks outside. It already looks abandoned after what seems like only a few days. My confidence that this will all end soon falters by the second.

We try to sleep a bit, but have far too much adrenaline coursing through our veins, and by two AM we're all raring to go. We all creep along the corridor and make it to the door unnoticed.

We manage to get outside without causing too much of a racket. My breath catches in my throat when the door clicks shut; I'm so certain we're going to get caught. We tip toe over to the wall, trying to keep as low as possible. I'm just praying to myself that Jake is right, and we can't be seen by cameras here. It's silly really. It's not as if they're not going to notice were missing, just because they can’t see us on film.

As we reach the bottom of the wall, I look up. It suddenly looks massive, far too big to get over. I start to freak out, but am stopped from saying anything by the site of Jake already giving Michelle a boost up. How are they so calm? They just knew to do that without even thinking or speaking. She hoists herself to the top and pulls herself over. I hear a loud tear as she falls to the ground. I bet she didn't think to pack any spare clothes and will now want mine.

Then it's my turn. I hoist myself up onto Jake's hands in such an embarrassing, ungainly fashion. I'm red faced and panting and I try to reach the top of the wall. I let out a little giggle at what I would have thought about this just a few short weeks ago, when my main goal was to impress Jake, which causes me to almost fall down the other side.

I have no idea how Jake manages to get over the wall without someone to help him, but he does about a second after I've landed. His face instantly goes pale when he looks up, and I follow his eye line. That's when I see Michelle's leg. Yes, her trousers tore as she went over the other side, but from the pool of blood gathering at her feet, she also hurt herself, badly. I start to feel dizzy. Blood has never been my strong point, and now my best friend is bleeding loads and we can't exactly call an ambulance to help her.

"Shit." Michelle only just realises herself. I guess the shock stopped her feeling the pain. She starts to hobble over to the other side of the street quickly.

"Wait!" I cry throwing my bag onto the ground "Bandages. We need to—"

I look around frantically and am silenced. In my peripheral vision, I can see about eight or nine infected people loitering about. And now, because of the racket I just made, they're all looking this way and starting to move in our direction. For a moment, I'm stunned. They seem weird. Inhuman and gross. Dirty and wasting away. I can't see any emotion in any of their faces, they're all just blank. Why are they all outside? I know, it's obvious they're all infected, just look at them. But, you'd think they'd hide or something, not just be stood, waiting to be killed. It's crazy, it's almost like there's just nothing left.

We run as fast as we can. Michelle's injury slows us down a bit, but luckily they don't seem to be able to move too fast. We detour around the back of houses, through fields, trying to get out of sight. We eventually stumble across a shed on someone's land. It's huge and there's no one about to see us so we slip inside. We patch up Michelle's leg as best we can with what we've got. I can't believe I didn't think to pick up antibiotics. Everyone knows they help with pretty much anything. They definitely would have warded off infection for a few days until Michelle can get some proper care.

She seems woozy, but I'm sure it's just from blood loss. A good night's sleep will sort that out. All my bravado has evaporated. It's easy to feel invincible when you're locked inside a nice warm building, with everything you need on tap. Now, faced with the harsh reality of the decision we've made, I'm a lot less sure. In fact, I'm certain we've made a mistake. I'm going to be responsible for even more deaths. In all our planning, and all my anal note writing, general injuries didn't even enter my imagination. How naive am I? And more importantly, what else have I forgotten to consider? Suddenly, five days seems a very long time.

# NINETEEN

The night seems to go on forever. It's so cold, and damp, I don't understand, it was warm earlier. The layers I had on were plenty, now they feel paper thin. My blanket is not even slightly helping. I can hear the wind howling as I'm drifting in and out of sleep, and the noise infiltrates my nightmares. All my fears come to the surface in my subconscious.

I dream that I'm surrounded by the infected. They're coming at me from every angle and there's no escape. Their faces, covered in scars and gore, limbs missing and the unmistakable stench of rot. Why do they smell that way? Like I imagine death smells. I turn round and round, trying to get away, trying to find a solution. I can't breathe as they get closer, my throat is constricted. I'm desperate for air. I can't think, can't concentrate. If only my vision wasn't blurring, I could decide what to do next.

I jolt awake, covered in sweat. Knowing there's no way I'll get back to sleep now. I sit awake and think. I'm grateful that we actually have a shelter over our heads tonight. Something to separate us from them. That is definitely not going to be the case every night. The more I think about this journey, the crazier I think we are. I don't even try to stop the tears from rolling down my cheeks.

My thoughts turn to my parents. I hope they're ok, I hope Felix took my advice and got them to stay indoors to keep them safe. I'm starting to get worried about what I'll find when I get there, if I make it of course. I take out my mobile, thinking that maybe I should text them to warn them I'm on my way, so they won't be too freaked when I arrive at their door. But of course I can't. Out of battery. Typical. I can't believe of everything I did think to do, charging my mobile wasn't one of them. Mind you, signal has been getting worse over the last few days, so maybe it wouldn't have worked anyway.

I almost wish I had told Felix what I was doing before we left. I didn't want to frighten him so I just kept my communication really basic. His was the same, no detail, just 'everything's fine.'

When the light starts to shine through the wooden slats, the others give up trying to sleep and we discuss our plan for the day. We know we have to be wary, we have no idea if were being hunted down, if work have reported us missing yet. I don't know the best way for us to go, or how far we should try and make it today. Michelle seems a bit better today, but she's very quiet, hardly contributing to our conversation, and when she stands up, it is obvious she's still in pain. Jake keeps glancing over to her, but does not stop talking. He's desperately trying to be positive, to boost our morale a bit. It's a good job he's here, to be honest, because if me and Michelle were alone right now, we'd go to bits, probably try and get back into the office. I have no doubt Jamie would not let us back in, frightened we would bring the infection with us, risking everyone else.

I wonder how mad he is right now. I bet he's livid. I can just picture him, pacing up and down, ranting about how irresponsible we are. Threatening the others not to do the same. I highly doubt any of us have a job to go back to. Fear hits me at that thought, like a punch in the stomach. What happens if this is all under control in two weeks? We are going to look like idiots. Unemployed idiots at that.

Oh God, that's really the least of any of our worries right now. It's more important to concentrate on living. Not getting attacked by any infected, or starving to death.

While I'm worrying, and getting myself all tied into knots, Jake decides he's going to go outside and scout the area, see if it's safe. While he's gone, we sit in silence. I stare at Michelle, trying to gauge how she's feeling. When I finally speak, just to ask her if she's ok, she doesn't answer, doesn't even look at me. She must blame me. There's no other explanation. I'm the one who stupidly insisted on this journey. If I had just ignored her that night, let her just rant on and took it for fear or madness, she wouldn't be in this mess now. Injured and at a huge risk. If I'd just taken this lockdown for exactly as it's supposed to be, a fortnight of staying indoors while the government deal with the infection, I wouldn't be outside in the freezing cold, frightened to death.

Finally, Michelle looks at me with shiny eyes and lets out a weak giggle. "I think we're going to be fine, you know," she says wistfully. Ok she's acting strange. I'm starting to worry that maybe she is starting to lose it, that her wound is infected somehow. "We got out of that hell hole, no problem. It's not that far to home," she continues, still smiling. "Jamie is going to freak. Oh well, I hated that job anyway."

Just as I'm about to respond, Jake's head pops around the door and he tells us to get a bloody move on right now.

When we get outside, I can see why Jake was so insistent that we move that instant. The infected are all about the place, just far enough away that we can walk along without too much concern, but they're starting to move towards us, so any longer and we would have had a problem. I suddenly notice Jake has picked up an axe that was in the corner of the shed. That's clever—I didn't even think to get something.

Jake see's me looking and says, "I just needed something to feel safe, so I can protect you two if needs be." Wow, that's really sweet. It's nice to know someone is there to care about us.

...

We've been walking across fields for hours. We've managed to avoid the roads so far, thinking that if we are the cause of a search party, the authorities will use cars.

Michelle is definitely slowing us down. She isn't talking about it, but her wound is really getting to her. With no pain killers to help, there's not a lot we can do. Jake is constantly on edge because of this. He wants to speed up, but knows it would be incredibly insensitive to mention it. I can feel the tension burning off both of them, and can sense I'm in the middle of a silent war. I keep trying to make conversation, to avoid the subject, but am not getting much response.

I'm about to address the situation, to insist that we are roughing this journey out together, no man left behind, and all that. I'm planning the argument in my head, when Jake indicates that we all crouch down, and keep quiet. My heart is racing as I'm straining to hear what he does. I'm certain we're about to be attacked by infected and am trying to signal to Jake that we need to move, not stay still. Then I hear voices. Other people are alive and outside. I'm so excited at the prospect of other law breakers like us, people that might have medication for Michelle, weapons and advice for us about our journey. I start to stand and cry out when Jake grabs me and shoves his hand over my mouth roughly. I look at him in shock. He's shaking his head at me.

When my anger at his actions subside, I realise he's right. I pull his hand off my face, indicating that I understand. Of course that isn't going to be people like us blatantly stood around talking. Not unless they're idiots. It'll be someone from the armed forces, or paramedics. Someone from the authorities that, as of a few days ago have been ordered to kill anyone they find outside on sight. I can't believe how close I was to putting us all in the firing line.

We stay crouched down, hidden for ages. It feels like an hour, but in reality is probably about 15 minutes. The voices continue, getting louder and louder. We can't make out what is being said, it's all too muffled, but it seems to be turning into a heated argument. Just as I'm starting to get really terrified were going to get found out, the shouting begins. Really loud yelling, like the people just don't care what they're going to attract. Then scuffling, it sounds like a fight is breaking out. I'm physically shaking now, frightened of how this is all going to end.

Eventually, the noise starts to subside. I sit frozen, holding my breath, willing my heart not to beat so loudly, but thinking maybe it's all over and they've moved on to another location. Just as I start to relax my shoulders, a gunshot rings out. A yelp passes my lips before I can stop it. Michelle and Jake both snap round to stare at me, eyes wide open. I slap my hands over my mouth, panicked. How the hell did I let that happen? Now we're absolutely going to be killed.

We stay silent and still, willing every second to pass with us unseen. I can't hear anyone rustling round, looking for us, but you never can tell. Eventually, to my utmost relief, we hear a car engine roaring and driving off. We must be closer to a road than we realised. Once we can no longer hear the vehicle, we stand up, still silent, and still wary. None of us really know what to say. Michelle powers on forward, determined to find out what happened, her leg forgotten temporarily in the flurry of activity.

Jake and I rush after her, scared of what she might find. Someone might still be there, in which case she's putting us all in grave danger. When we get through the bushes, we find out there has been someone left behind. A body is lying on the floor covered in blood. Well, that's the gunshot explained. I can't help wondering what got this guy killed. Was it just an argument got out of hand, or was he killed by a government official? If so, that's just cold blooded murder. I know that's their job and they have to follow instructions, but don't they feel any guilt? This guy was talking, probably quite coherently. I don't understand his skin isn't greying like the others I have seen, he hasn't got any bite marks. In fact his only injury is the gun shot.

I suddenly notice a tugging on my sleeve. Jake. He's trying to communicate something to me silently, why doesn't he just speak? It can't exactly be a secret from Michelle, whatever he's trying to say. I look around and see we have a few guests coming along to join our party. The noise of the gun must have attracted their attention. And now they've spotted us, which has just piqued their interest. Luckily they're very slow, so we manage to escape, leaving them to the guy that's just been killed. I feel bad letting them at him like that, I wouldn't like that to happen to me, even in the case of my death, but if it keeps us three alive I can't really complain too much.

I make the fatal error of turning back, just to check they have been distracted enough to leave us alone. What a mistake that is. The infected are all feasting on that poor man. This shouldn't be too much of a shock, I did see what happened to Tom, but the way they're pulling him to bits, dragging out his intestines, it's revolting. I know he's already dead but to see him torn apart as if by wild animals. AM13 is not like any other virus or disease I've ever seen. There's something really different about it, the way it seems to turn people into empty shells of themselves, slaves to a weird hunger that turns them into cannibals, unable to even control themselves. It's not right. It's definitely not natural. Maybe the people online, who said it was a government weapon to control population weren't nut jobs. They had it right all along. If that's the case, the scientist that invented AM13, did a bloody good job. Too good.

I turn away, disgusted, and jog to catch up to the others. I run for as long as I can, before I have to stop, and throw up all the contents of my stomach. Luckily, I guess, there isn't much in there since we skipped out on breakfast.

The whole day is spent walking, pretty much in silence, trying to digest the events of this morning in our own way. We have done well at keeping hidden, from everyone, by keeping off the road as much as possible and hiding in small lanes and backstreets where necessary. Now it is starting to get dark and we are all very tired and hungry. Especially Michelle, who is looking worse by the minute. Sweat is dripping down her face and neck and she looks very red and stressed out. The blood is leaking through the bandage on her leg, and

I start to worry that she might not make it through all this in one piece.

"We need to find somewhere to rest soon," I quickly decide and Michelle looks over to me gratefully. She's obviously wanted to say this for a while, but must have been worried we'd think she was weak because of her leg. Luckily there's no argument from Jake. In fact he's sure he knows of a warehouse nearby where we can sleep safely. It's the stock room of a large clothing company, so it will definitely be abandoned during the lockdown. There's no way the boss of that sort of business could have justified keeping them all at work. And if we're lucky, we can get a change of clothes and layer up better.

It's not too much of a walk, which we're all incredibly thankful for, and Jake manages to break us in without too much hassle. The alarm goes off briefly, but he smashes the controls to pieces with his axe, which silences it very effectively. I can't help thinking we're going to owe this company a lot of money, if we don't end up in prison as soon as the lockdown is lifted. I guess security isn't the top priority at the moment, companies probably think a fortnight inside isn't going to lead to much looting or vandalism. After a quiet dinner of canned fruit and vegetables, and a last minute check that all the doors are secure, we all find somewhere to settle down and sleep, far too tired to talk, or even think.

I wake up early, refreshed after a much better, dreamless sleep. I must have been exhausted. Plus all the extra layers for warmth helped. I feel much more positive about what today will bring. It's amazing what a nice sleep and clean clothes can do. I decide to make everyone a half decent breakfast to wake up to, to help them both feel as optimistic as I do today. Who knows, maybe the lighter mood will help us travel further. I stand up and scan the room, and immediately notice something is wrong. Jake is still fast asleep, where I left him last night.

But Michelle is missing.

# TWENTY

Ok, don't panic. Do not freak out. If I just stay calm, everything will be ok. Deep breath. Ok, don't panic. I keep repeating this to myself while my insides dance about, completely ignoring my brain. She can't have gone too far I try to rationalise. She's left all her stuff here, and what with her injuries. She just would not go out alone without a bloody good reason. If only I could figure out what the hell her reason was. We've scanned the entire warehouse, and can't find any sign of Michelle, or any clue to where she might have gone.

Jake hasn't uttered one opinion to the situation. This puts me on edge; if he hasn't got anything to say, maybe it's because he thinks something bad has happened to her. No, I can't think like that. He's wrong, she's fine. I suddenly realise he's talking. He wants to search outside as we're not exactly having any luck here. There's no way he's going alone, leaving me by myself. What if something happens to him? Then I'll be left to face this with no one. I just can't let that happen. Plus, he's the only one with any kind of weapon.

We debate whether or not to leave our stuff behind, in case Michelle comes back while we're out. I think it's a good idea, so she doesn't think we've just up and left her, but Jake is firmly against it. We don't know what we could come back to find, and if the building is surrounded by the infected, or maybe someone, out like us, steals our supplies—there's always a small chance. Well, without them, we've literally got no chance of surviving. I grab Michelle's bag, and inside it find her mobile phone. Out of battery too, what a surprise. I decide to leave both her phone and mine in view as a little message, so she knows were coming back for her. She always used to joke that my mobile was practically glued to my hands, so hopefully she will understand what I mean. There's no way I'm leaving without her.

We stick close together, not daring to leave each other's side. Jake is scanning the area and whispering to me everything he can see, a few infected, not too close luckily, the odd animal, but nothing that's of use to me. I'm sure he's just talking to keep himself focused. My fingers are numb with the cold and I'm petrified for Michelle. What the hell is she thinking taking off on us like that? She knew we'd worry and come looking for her. What could be so important that she'd risk all of us?

We've covered all the area nearby, so decide we're going to have to make it out to the roads. There's a small business park not too far from here, which we passed yesterday. Maybe Michelle went there hunting for supplies. That's actually quite a reasonable explanation.

That's the sort of thing she would do, especially since I imagine she's thinking that she's holding us back, and not being useful. That's so typical of Michelle, she always has to be independent and in control, I bet she can't bear being a burden. Not that I think she's a burden of course. I'm starting to buck up a bit as we approach; I just know she's here. God, I'm going to tell her exactly how predictable she is when we finally see her.

...

"Michelle. Michelle!" I've given up trying to be quiet and am just yelling her name top volume. We have been searching here for absolutely ages with no luck. We've even broke into most of the buildings, just to check she isn't trapped. Nothing. We've stumbled across a few infected people. Obviously some people did try to hide inside buildings when they noticed early signs of the virus, but it looks like the predictions were correct—once it's in your blood stream you have no hope. Jake actually had to kill a couple of them as they tried to attack us. I looked away as he bought his axe down into them over and over. I shouted at him to make sure he got them in the head, but didn't check to see if he'd followed my advice. I know that if he hadn't killed them, we would have been bitten, but I just can't bear the thought of it.

I'm also desperately trying to ignore the blood covering us both. The smell is making my skin crawl. We must look like mass murderers, which doesn't help me deal with what we've done. I just sincerely hope we can get back into that warehouse later, and change out of these clothes.

The fear is gnawing in my stomach now. I just can't believe we haven't found her yet. What if something bad has happened to her? Possible scenarios are finally making their way into my brain. I've been trying to force them away all day, but now I can't stop them. What if she's been eaten? Or just bitten and decided to get away from us? Or what if she's been kidnapped? Or caught by the authorities? The only hole in all these theories is me and Jake. Why would any of these leave us behind?

The only other possibility is she was starting to go loopy with pain. What if she started to hallucinate and crawled off into a ditch somewhere? We'd have found her wouldn't we? We've looked pretty much everywhere. Oh God, I feel so awful.

Jake keeps trying to say something, but can't seem to find the words. I know exactly what it's going to be as well. He's going to tell me we've looked all day, everywhere possible, and shouted her name top volume. He's going to add that we've worn ourselves out, wasting a whole day of supplies by not progressing on our journey and another day of looking will be pointless. If we haven't found her by now, we never will. Before he opens his mouth again, I interrupt.

"No!" He looks startled "We have to stay, we can't just leave her. You know we can't. She's injured, and probably alone somewhere and frightened. With any luck she's probably back at the warehouse by now." He looks a bit discomforted at that. "She's my best friend. She would stay for me, and I'll stay for her. I know you want to go and get this journey over with, but we started it together and we should end it that way. If we leave her now, we give her no chance at surviving."

Jake knows that there's no way of changing my mind. I think a part of him is relieved, I doubt he could have really just heartlessly left her in these conditions. My heart sinks as we open the warehouse door. Still no sign. The mobile phones just sit there, exactly as I left them, taunting me. Frustrated tears prick my eyes. We eat in silence, before settling down to try and get some sleep. This time, we huddle together, both too scared and upset to face the dark alone.

I don't sleep a wink. Thoughts of Michelle just swirl round and round in my mind. I'm really trying so hard to think where or why she might have gone. I think back to our conversations before we left, planning our break out, giggling at our rebellious nature, trying to piece together a solution. It's then I realise, maybe she headed back to the office to try and get help, to get her leg sorted. It was pretty bad. That's why she left her bag, so Jake and I would have plenty of supplies. And she didn't tell us because she knew we'd go with her, which would put us way behind schedule. Plus if Jamie had let us in, we would never have got out again.

As much as I hope this is the truth, I still feel bad for Michelle. I hope she makes it in one piece. And I wish she'd told me. Yes, I would have gone back with her, but I wouldn't have minded. This journey is not exactly fun and she knows how important she is to me.

Oh God, I just hope she turns up tomorrow and we can put all this behind us. At least that way we'll know for sure what has happened.

# TWENTY-ONE

When the morning comes, there's still no sign of Michelle. I'm starting to feel really desperate now. Where the hell is she? She couldn't even leave some kind of note? I know we didn't exactly think to bring writing equipment, but she could have found something here if she looked hard enough. I just can't believe she'd leave us like this, with no clue about her whereabouts. I'd never do anything like this to her, ever.

Jake is starting to get antsy and hinting about leaving the warehouse behind. The infected are starting to move towards us. Maybe they can hear us, or maybe they can just smell us and are getting hungry. In any case, if we don't move soon, we'll get stuck. My determination about not leaving without Michelle is starting to waver. I'm not sure what choice we have. If we stay here, even just for one more night, we'll die. They'll get close enough to attack us for sure. And if she comes back and sees the building surrounded, she's not going to come in anyway is she?

I just don't want to become like them. I don't want to get attacked and end up milling about looking for the next human to munch on. I can't bear the thought of AM13 running through my veins, turning me into something else—something that is definitely not me. Something that is willing to maim and kill others, without even a second thought.

I know, it's the most selfish decision I could ever make, but I can't see any other option. I'm frightened and that is what is driving me to want to go.

All I can smell around me is death. I'm not sure if it's being surrounded by people riddled with the virus, organs shutting down one by one, until their only function is eating, or just fear of my own impending doom. I remember all the diagrams and drawings I saw online, detailing how AM13 takes over your body and mind. It's so different seeing it first hand, in real life.

I can't help but think, if only people had listened to the numerous warnings. If only people had followed the lockdown properly, they might not have ended up in the state they are now, where their only escape is death. If only everyone had believed straight away, there's no way it would have spread so quickly.

Mind you, who am I to talk? I supposedly found this virus and I didn't believe in it. That seems so long ago now, like a whole lifetime. In a few short days I already feel like a different person. All I was concerned about then was my stupid reputation. How unimportant that all seems compared to what I'm facing now. And here I am, despite everything I've seen and experienced, out in the open, disobeying the lockdown. Without Michelle.

I absently wonder how many others there are, like us. Outside, avoiding the authorities and the infected equally. Trying to get somewhere they should have gone before all this started. I hope if Michelle does bump into anyone, they look after her.

...

Jake is already packing up our things, eager to move on. The terror in his eyes is forcing his hand. I know he's still concerned about Michelle, I think he just couldn't cope with losing both of us. He's muttering to himself about which direction we should head in. One which will progress our journey, but will also cover any area we didn't get to yesterday, just in case.

Survival has become such a high priority. It always was really, but Michelle's disappearance has hit us both hard, and highlights all the dangers we'll probably have to face at some point. I think back to all our hushed meetings back in the little garden area, outside the office. I remember how, through all our discussions and planning, my main focus was subconsciously still trying to find a spark between me and him. How naive. If I'd only known.

I can feel a burning rage bubbling up, mixed with a huge sense of loss. I just feel so useless. A tear rolls down my cheek, just because my body doesn't know how else to react. I never once considered doing this without Michelle. I didn't think about any of us getting hurt either, or dying. Not really. Now I can't think about anything else.

Jake picks up Michelle's bag and I snatch it off him immediately.

"We're leaving this here." I say determinedly.

"But—"

"No buts. I know we could probably use the supplies. But we have to leave it, in case she comes back. It's the least we can do."

The look on my face tells Jake I won't budge, so he leaves it where it is. With both the mobiles. Just so she'll know. I want her to see how sorry I am. In fact, as soon as I get home, I'm going to make sure someone comes looking for her. I'll even phone the authorities. I'll explain it to them. Make them understand.

Angry tears continue to run down my cheeks. I wish they wouldn't, I hate being so pathetic. I don't even deserve to cry. I'm the one still here, safe. Michelle is the one that's lost.

Wordlessly Jake walks over to me and gestures at me to get up and go. I do so with a heavy heart. My whole body is coiling round in knots. I can't bring myself to say anything else, to vocalise what we're doing. I so wish there was any other way. But I'm no use to her dead. When I finally get her back, I'm going to do anything for her. I'll make up for this, if it's the last thing I do.

We trudge down to the road morosely, and after scouting the area and checking for Michelle, decide to carry on and walk alongside it. It's a very risky move, considering we might be seen, but it's so much quicker than the alternative. We need to make up for lost time. We only have enough food with us to last a few days.

The only words we exchange are about the journey, where to go next, how to avoid everyone. We even consider stealing a car, but the noise will attract them and we have a much higher chance of being caught by the authorities. Both options lead to dying, so aren't really preferable.

We eventually reach the edge of a small housing estate, which leads on to a little street of shops. The first thing I notice is how derelict things have become. It's a huge shock, and I find myself wondering again if we have actually been going through this for years, rather than a few weeks. Litter covers the streets, and the only sounds I can hear is that of small scurrying animals, grabbing all the food they can. I feel weird. Empty and lost. This can't be reality, it just can't.

We discuss what to do, scared we'll be reported if anyone sees us. I wonder aloud what the chances are of someone offering us a hot meal, or even a bed for the night if we knock on their door, but Jake instantly shoots down that idea.

"Imagine how terrified these people are. They have probably all seen an attack first hand, now they're all locked indoors with only the TV for company, forcing fear further down their throats. No way will anyone risk their family. We could be infected for all they know."

Of course he's right, but it would have been so nice to have a peaceful sleep, in a bed. We decide to sneak down to the parade of shops, and see if we can break into any of those. Just for shelter and hopefully for some food. We really are running lower than we should be already.

The possible pros outweigh the cons, so we decide to go for it. While were creeping down the road, I try and sneak a look in peoples windows, just to see if anyone looks friendly. If not to let us in, maybe just to let me use the phone. If I could ring the office. Jamie would verbally murder me, but I could also ask if Michelle is there, just so I'd know.

Even if they hadn't seen her, I could get some help. Damn, now that's all I want to do. Why are there no pay phones anywhere anymore? Mind you, I have no change with me anyway, didn't think I'd have a reason to use it.

Looking in through everyone's window isn't proving to be the threat I thought it would. I was expecting many suspicious eyes, trying to find out if were infected and what we're up to. But not one person has spotted us. No one seems to even be looking outside. We could probably just walk along normally, unnoticed. But we still don't take that risk. I guess with nothing good to see, just poor people in the grips of the virus occasionally milling about, what's the point in even opening the curtains? It's easier to pretend the horrors of the outside don't exist from inside your home.

There's not a lot of noise coming from any of the houses. I'm not sure if people are just too bored to do anything loud, or if they've just learnt that noise attracts the infected. No one wants their house to be surrounded. God, I wish I was at home already. I wish I'd just done what I wanted and left in the first place. Why did I let

Jamie manipulate me? I wouldn't be in this mess now.

One house stops me in my tracks. A family are standing at the window, a mother, father and daughter by the looks of it. They're all infected. Obviously one of them had it, and instead of turning them in, they hid them. It was probably the child. No one would willingly hand over their children to God knows who. An overwhelming sadness hits me. I wonder how many other houses are the same—full of infected because families risked themselves rather than giving a loved one up to the authorities. I'm surprised they haven't been killed yet. The armed forces must have noticed them when doing the rounds. Why have they just left them? Maybe because inside, they can't get to anyone else so they aren't a priority. Or maybe they're slowly losing control of the situation. How would we know? Stuck out here with no way to access the news. The thought makes me shudder, this needs to end sometime.

Jake is quiet. I can tell by the haunted look in his eyes, he's thinking of his son. He must be so frightened that Harry is in the same state. Without thinking, I open my mouth.

"How do you cope? Deal with what you've done? Killing them back there?" Idiot. What a thing to say at a time like this. What is my brain to mouth filter playing at?

He answers defensively. "Well, I don't exactly think I killed them. They were already dead. I just put them out of their misery." I look up at him surprised so he carries on. "None of their normal organs are functioning, they're behaving like cannibals. They shuffle about slowly, blankly, no sign of human emotion or memory. People have bitten their own children. Do you think that they're still classed as 'alive'? They're already dead, plain and simple. And to be quite frank, if I was in that condition, risking other people's lives, I'd want someone to smash an axe through my head, too."

I'm silent for a long time after Jake's rant, thinking. Everything he says makes a lot of sense, and to be quite honest, it makes the whole thing a lot easier to think of that way. If they're already dead, we did do them a favour. I just hope I don't end up that way, but I know now Jake will do the right thing if I do. What a depressing thought. The *right thing.* I desperately hope it does not come to that.

I question Jake on the possibility of a cure. Without one I don't see this ever ending. I can't see them getting to every single infected person, people will always hide. Even if they do, they can't stop it from coming back here. Especially without any information on what caused it. Jake thinks there probably are people working on it, but whenever it was raised back at work, to experts and people supposedly in the know, the answers always skirted around the issue and just blinded viewers with science. That's not at all reassuring—if there is no answer, there's no hope.

We soon reach the street of shops. It's so empty. It looks so weird without any shoppers, like a ghost town. I didn't exactly expect anything different, but it's still strange. The shops all feel really familiar, and they remind me of before. Of my old life. Of popping out to the shops on a Saturday to buy a little something, despite not really having any money. Of heading to the supermarket after work to get something in for dinner. Of worrying that I might not be able to pass off my second hand clothes as new at work, trying to impress my colleagues who always seemed so much more glamorous than me. Funny how much time I spent worrying about the opinions of all the people I just walked away from without even a second glance. How ironic that when it comes down to it, I don't really care about any of them.

Except Michelle of course, but if I think about her too much I'll break down. I need to wait until we're at least inside somewhere safe, where I don't need my wits 100% about me, before I can let that happen. I do really wish we'd stayed at the warehouse.

The food shop shelves are almost empty. I guess they have either already been looted, or everything was bought before the lockdown began. It seems the shop owners didn't bother to restock, just to leave it all to go off. To my utter distaste, I notice many of them were running 'End of the World Sales'. Really classy. That's just mocking and taking advantage of a bad situation, even if they didn't really realise the true extent of the truth. Although, in a way, it's no different to what Jamie did at the news station to up our ratings and further our careers.

We eventually come across one small corner shop which doesn't have any sale signs on display. It's still stocked much better than the others, which is good news for us, so we decide to break into this one and shelter for the night. Good a place as any. We start to force the door open as quietly as possible. We can never guarantee that we're alone, and we don't want to put ourselves in line of any danger.

Finally a click and a snapping sound, we're in. I grin and Jake and I rush forward. Chocolate, so much wonderful chocolate. You don't realise how much you'll miss it until it's gone. I peel open a wrapper and scarf the bar so quickly, you'd think I hadn't eaten for months. The taste is so sweet and heavenly; it brings my taste buds alive and forms a contented warm feeling in my stomach. I look over to Jake.

He's frozen still, on the spot. He hasn't grabbed a single thing to eat and he must be starving. I know I am. My instincts tell me to walk over to him, to find out what has got him so worried. I creep over to him slowly, trying not to make any noise. I suddenly feel sick with fear. All I want to do is grab Jake and hide behind him, while we get as far away from here as possible.

The feeling of unease suddenly explodes, when I see what Jake is looking at. The shop owner. Stood there, right in front of us. How the hell did I not see him before? I open my mouth to apologise, to tell him I'll pay for the food, to convince him we're not infected. My mind is running ten to the dozen, trying to figure out what I should say first. He shuffles forward, his age obviously slowing him down. I back away.

When he steps into the light, I understand. There's no point in saying anything. Nothing will work. He's no longer human. He's infected. He's dead.

# TWENTY-TWO

He's disgusting. I've never seen one this close before, heading towards me, I've always managed to avert my eyes, but now time seems to freeze as I can't drag my gaze away. What I thought was him shuffling, was actually him dragging his broken, bloodied leg behind him. The wound is so deep, I can see bone. I retch.

The bite on his shoulder is huge. His arm is hanging down by his side, useless. He'll never be able to move that again, no matter what happens. His face is also in a terrible state. His skin is a deep grey, much murkier than the others I've seen. He must have been infected for a long time. The bags under his eyes droop incredibly low, causing his face to look deformed. The blood running down his face, staining all his clothes looks old, almost black. Scratch marks cover his torso; he looks as if he's been brutally beaten in some awful fight. I would never have thought someone could survive these injuries. People have died over much less, and yet here he is, moving towards us, baring his teeth.

Jake pulls me hard and I stumble backwards, tripping over a box. I can't move. I feel like I'm having an out of body experience, looking down at myself, screaming *run.* Something is pulling me up, but my body is sluggish. It just won't do what I want it to, I'm too panicked. Now I know how Tom was feeling when he was attacked. Limp and useless. I know an assault is imminent, but I can't do anything to stop it. I'm screwed.

I'm shaking, sobs rising up in my chest. I'm going to die if I don't move, so why can't I? All I need to do is get to the door, but it feels a million miles away. I don't even know where Jake is. I can hear him hissing at me, encouraging me to move, but I can't see him anywhere. He might have even made it outside already.

Thud. The loud noise shocks me into looking up. Thud. There it is again. This time it's following by a sloshing sound, like a wet mop hitting the ground. I need to locate the source of the noise. I need to know what's happening, how long I have left. Can I escape?

Jake, I can see him. He's covered in blood. His axe is lying on the ground next to him. He's offering me a hand.

"He's...?" I can't finish my sentence.

"Yes Leah, he's gone."

Relief floods my chest, pushing away some of the numb sensation. I have never had a near death experience before, so I'm not sure how you're supposed to feel.

We sit silent for a while, just the sounds of our heavy breathing to keep us company. The shop owner doesn't move again, so I'm starting to relax. I wonder what happened to him, how he managed to get into that state.

Jake instructs me to grab as much food as I can carry, to try and stock up on enough to get us all the way home, so we don't have to go through anything like this again. I know we could probably stay here now, but neither of us considers it. I don't think my heart could take another close call like that.

...

We decide to carry on walking, as it's not quite pitch black yet, and get as far away from any buildings as possible. Anywhere that was heavily populated before seems to bring a higher risk of bumping into the infected. I guess if they haven't been given a good reason to move on from wherever they get attacked, they don't.

We walk for another hour, until it gets too dark to see and we come across a park area. I'm not keen on spending the night out in the open. I feel too exposed. At least inside we have four walls surrounding us, keeping the infected away. I'm terrified, but I don't see any other option. I'm freezing and far too tense to sleep. I have no idea what we're going to do next. Every time I attempt to close my eyes all I can see is faces—Tom, the man from the shop, the woman who attacked the biker, Michelle. Always Michelle. What happened to you Michelle? Why did you leave me? I wish I'd stayed to find out what happened, but I was scared. You must understand that, and you might never have come back. Then what would have happened to me? I know I'm making excuses for an inexcusable action. I'm sorry. I wish I'd never left. I just hope you're safe somewhere, being looked after.

I don't think Jake gets much sleep either. As soon as the sun starts to rise, we both instantly sit up and get ready to move. I don't think I've ever been so cold, even my bones feel chilly. As there is currently no one in sight, we decide to quickly eat before walking again.

Damn it, we have no vegetarian stuff left. I mustn't have brought enough for myself in all the rushing. I haven't eaten meat in 15 years, and never wanted to, but it looks like I'm going to have to start if I don't want to starve.

The meat balls I'm eating are revolting. I'm definitely reverting back to veggie as soon as I have options again. If I wasn't so hungry, and didn't have so much travelling to do today, I'd leave it. Jake is laughing at me gagging on each bite, telling me beggars can't be choosers. Well, I'm glad I'm a source of amusement to someone.

When we start walking again, Jake starts to talk. Probably to fill the silence more than anything. He tells me about Harry, about how much he loves his son. I listen, glad of the distraction. Eventually I start to worry—I hope he isn't telling me all this because he thinks we aren't going to make it. I need him to be positive to keep me going. It's his determination that's got us this far.

That's when I make a pledge to myself. No matter what happens, I'm going to get Jake to his son. I'm going to make sure he finds them, and gets to know what has happened. Hopefully they'll be fine, just holed up somewhere safe. His needs on this journey are much greater than mine. I'll make sure he survives this. I can't make up for what I did to Michelle, but I can do this. I can put Jake and Harry before myself. I have to.

When he starts discussing our next moves, I nod and agree with everything he says. To be honest, he's much better at taking control of the situation that I am anyway, I think I've proven that in the past. I've always just sat back, and let things happen to me, then when it all goes wrong, I wallow in self-pity and hope it all goes away. Look at how I reacted to this virus story being leaked under my name.

We are going to carry on along this road, until we find some kind of service station. Then we're going to spend the night there. Jake is keen, as am I, to not spend another night outside. It was much too frightening. A petrol station will be filled with things we need, food, water, blankets, plus it'll be inside, a safe place to sleep. Protected.

# TWENTY-THREE

We've been moving for hours with no break. Damn how I wish I'd used my gym membership more. I was never there, and think how useful that extra fitness would have been to me now. We've been walking alongside the road, but near to the hedge so we can jump in them to hide at a moment's notice. We haven't seen any infected for a while now. And as I'm thinking about it, I realise we haven't heard any cars either, or seen any people. Must be luck. I would have thought they'd be out constantly, clearing out every area of people with the virus. Maybe this place has been completely cleared? Plus, I've seen no food deliveries; maybe there aren't really any houses around here?

Being on the run sucks. Now I know how escaped convicts feel; constantly vigilant, looking over their shoulders, no security, no consistent source of food or water, no washing/eating/sleeping when you feel like it.

As we pass fields, I try to ignore all the animals. They're wasting away, it's awful. Maybe no one is feeding them now they can't go outside. Some of them are bloody and almost dying. Maybe the infected are also eating them? They're eating humans; I suppose it only makes sense. It's a familiar food source to most people, they must recognise the smell. I've not seen any of that happening, and I don't remember it being said in all the reams of information we gave out on the news. Who knows? The best thing I can do is try not to think about it. The thought of them attacking poor defenceless animals makes me feel ill.

Hours later, we finally come across what were looking for—a small petrol station. It's just on the brink of getting dark, so it's really perfect timing. Petrol stations seem to be absolutely everywhere when you're driving along, but my God they're so far apart when you're walking. I doubt we'd see another one tonight. There are cars littered around the pumps, as if people were stockpiling diesel. That must just be an instinctive reaction in any kind of panic. People are predictable. What I don't understand is why the cars are still here. Surely the people driving them, would have also taken them home? Or at least onto wherever the hell they were going?

"What happened here?" I ask Jake. He looks just as confused as me.

"It appears as if everyone may have dumped their cars trying to escape something. Whatever it is I just hope it's not here now."

We immediately hear a low groaning sound, which gets my hackles rising. That noise is familiar. It reminds me of the shop owner, of the buildings on that business estate, of the attack on Tom, which can only mean one thing.

My heart is pounding loudly as were crouching down on the ground. I'm certain it's going to get us discovered. I might as well be screaming for all the noise it's making. My fear leaves a weird metallic taste in my mouth, and I just can't think straight to know what to do. I'd be absolutely useless alone. I'm so glad to have Jake here. He seems so calm, so focused. His eyes are flicking in every direction, trying to locate the source of the sound so we can avoid that direction. I look at him in admiration. It's incredible how good he is in stressful situations. He should be in the army or something. His talents are wasted at the station.

"Oh, it's ok," he finally says and stands up "The groaning is coming from here." He points at a car. Inside is an infected woman, desperately clawing at the window to get to us. She can't move because she's trapped by her seat belt. She doesn't have the intelligence left to realise that's what's pinning her down. She obviously can't remember how to take a seat belt off. Wow, the reports that the brain function is one of the quickest to go must be right.

She looks so pathetic, it makes me sad. Someone must have bought an infected person here, maybe wanting to drive them away somewhere safe, but the virus took hold and they started to attack people. I start to think how I can't believe people would leave anyone behind, how selfish, until Michelle's face floods my mind, and that hollow feeling in my stomach returns.

I can just picture the scene of the attacks here. It's almost as if it's happening in front of my eyes. The screaming, the blood, the running, the yelling, the sheer panic. It must have been horrendous for people to run, leaving their cars behind. Hopefully most people managed to escape. If every single person from these cars was caught, and bitten—that just doesn't bear thinking about. There were probably children, and elderly.

I tell Jake that we have to do it. We have to put her out of her misery. It would be inhumane to leave her here, like that, stuck and no longer able to do anything for herself. Plus if a miracle occurred and she did manage to get out, we'd be putting ourselves in danger. I know he resents me for saying it, because he knows I don't intend to do it myself, that I want him to do the dirty work of killing her, but that doesn't stop him. He knows I'm right. He opens the car door and uses his axe to finish her off. I just squeeze my eyes shut, and try to hum a tune in my head, because I can't bear to see it. I know, I'm pathetic. I'm useless.

...

Breaking into the building isn't too hard considering the door is just left unlocked. I guess whoever was on duty had to escape too, without thinking too much about ensuring all the security features were set. We search everywhere before relaxing, and don't find a single person. What a relief. It seems things might be starting to go our way a little bit. We find some edible food, which is great because it means we don't have to break into our supplies, and Jake finds some alcohol stashed in the office.

Ok, so drinking might not be the wisest decision considering everything that's going on. Our reactions will be affected tonight, plus I don't exactly relish the idea of a stinking hangover tomorrow, but after everything we've been through in the past few days, there's no way we could not drink it.

We get very tipsy, to the point of hysterical laughter. It feels nice to blow off a bit of steam. To block out the outside world and the horrors that come with it. We talk about everything else possible—our lives growing up, our families, even people back at the office. The only subject we really avoid is Michelle. That would just be a huge dampener on the first happy evening since all this began.

After the third bottle of wine, which I notice is disappearing very quickly, I start to spot a glint forming in Jake's eye. One that I have only seen once before. I start to realise where this night is headed, and just in time too, because before I know it, his mouth is on mine, his hands everywhere. Is this really a good idea? Now? Tonight? With all that's going on? I mean, we haven't exactly washed properly for days. This sort of thing usually takes a lot of planning, a lot of grooming and nice underwear. I don't think I've ever let it happen so spontaneously before.

And then I just shut my mind off and let my body do the thinking for me.

# TWENTY-FOUR

The next morning we wake up naked, our bodies entwined with each other. If this were normal circumstances, I would now be rushing to the bathroom to make myself look presentable. I'd be trying to apply as much natural looking make up as possible while dragging a brush through my hair. I'd even try and squeeze in a quick shower, and I'd definitely brush my teeth. I'd also be analysing every tiny detail from last night in my mind. I'd be worrying that I'd said something dumb. Most of all I'd be trying to work out whether it was just a drunken thing, or could it turn into more. But this morning, I don't have any of these options available to me, so instead I just lie there and enjoy the blissful feeling.

I'm suddenly aware that Jake is trying to sit up, but I'm in the way. I move then turn to smile at him, but he looks really sheepish, as if he wants to say something uncomfortable. The contentment zaps straight out of me. I know that expression and the conversation that follows it and it certainly isn't wedding planning. I know I have no right to be pissed off, I mean we aren't exactly in a position to discuss a relationship, considering we have no idea what could happen tomorrow, or even in five minutes. I just can't help feeling a bit used. I throw my clothes on and mumble about searching for anything we can use today. My face is flaming red and I don't want him to see, so I go out into the back.

That's when I notice a rickety door that I'm sure we didn't look behind yesterday. I guess with it being dark we just didn't see it. I grab a nearby plank of wood, just in case. I open the door cautiously, desperate to know what lies behind it, and hoping it's not full of infected. I don't think a bit of wood is going to be much use to me if there is. Curiosity really could kill the cat.

"I've found a shower," I yell out to Jake. "A shower with real life hot running water!" He chases in behind me, obviously unable to trust my words. "I'm going in first." I sing out excitedly. He laughs at my elation. Never in my life have I been so glad to see a shower. I grab shampoo, conditioner and shower gel and dive in. The boiling water running over my skin makes me feel rejuvenated and much more positive about the journey ahead. I don't even really care so much about Jake's behaviour this morning. It could have easily been my own paranoia. I just need to stop taking a negative stance.

...

Once we have both washed and eaten, we become much more smiley and chatty with each other. Any awkwardness from this morning completely forgotten. We pack up, ready to go, almost with a skip in our step, such a difference to yesterday. I'm just doing one last scan of the office, when a glint of metal catches my eye. A gun. Just lying there on the floor, tucked under the desk. It must belong to the petrol station and has been dropped. If only I had any idea how to use one, it would be so useful right about now.

I hand it over to Jake, and ask him if he thinks we should bring it. He opens it up to look inside and tells me there is some ammo in it, so we might as well. You never know if we may need it. I don't ask him if he knows what to do with it, I don't want to know. I'll just feel safer knowing it's there, tucked in Jake's bag.

We head outside, and the sun is almost shining. It's a lot warmer than yesterday in any case. Just as I'm about to say that I really think today will be a good one, we hear a scream, followed by a shout, and footsteps, running. I freak out, and duck behind a car, desperate to keep out of sight. Jake follows me and I look at him questioningly. What the hell is going on now? Suddenly I'm deafened by gun shots, lots of them. I glance up trying to see through the car window what is happening. I can see a boy, running, begging and pleading. Insisting he's fine, nothing has got to him, He's not infected. Whoever he's trying to tell is still firing at him, so either they can't hear him, or they're just ignoring his every word.

He falls to the ground, but the shots don't stop. A man wearing a protective suit that covers every inch of his body walks over to the boy, kicks him, before firing one last shot into his head. He then drags him into the back of a parked van. Jake pulls me under the car, alongside him, and we watch the van driving away. A police riot van.

I collapse into sobs. The brutality of that boy's murder was incredible. He didn't look much older than Felix, and he definitely did not look infected. He had no signs of an attack or anything. That could happen to us, so easily. Again I'm sent back to what the hell were we thinking? Jake just throws his arm around me and waits for the crying to subside.

When the tears stop, we move out from under the car, and start walking. No words are exchanged between us. There's no need. What can we say? We both know how the other is feeling and we just need to concentrate on getting through this. My eyes don't leave the ground once. I'm just watching my feet going through the motion of walking, of just going forward.

I'm listening to the motion of our feet. We are walking in unison, so I'm sure Jake is doing the same. It's silly, considering constant awareness is really a priority, but the noise is something positive. It represents us moving, getting somewhere. It's focusing on this that causes us to miss out on something vital. Squelching, shuffling, moaning. By the time either of us realises that the noises have gotten closer, it's too late. They're already on us.

There's about seven or eight right behind us. I'm running faster than I ever have before. I didn't realise my legs had so much power in them. It just shows that adrenaline really can cause you to be able to do crazy things. Jake is just ahead of me, but he keeps turning around to check I'm ok. My breaths are getting shorter and shorter. I'm suddenly really aware that I can't do this for much longer. It's just lucky for me that they're so slow, which gives me a minute to make a decision.

A tree. My instincts tell me to climb it. Jake is far ahead and he doesn't seem to show any signs of lagging so I just go for it. I jump up and once I'm on a steady branch, too high up for anything to grab me, I call out his name. I know that noise isn't exactly great in this situation, but I can't really see how it can get much worse. Jake turns around and I let out a sigh of relief and motion for him to carry on, at least he knows I'm safe. That's all I wanted to do.

But then he doubles back around and starts running to where I am. What is he doing? I wave my arms and shake my head at him. No that's not what I wanted, he needs to save himself. He's just dashing straight back into danger now. He waves his axe out in front of him, trying to knock a few out of the way as he gets closer. They're starting to surround the tree, the smell of my freshly cleaned skin drawing them in.

He struggles to get past them. I'm biting down on my nails hard. This is terrible. This is exactly why I didn't want him to come back to get me, I'm calling out. Trying to help, but everything I do just seems to make it worse. They're pulling on his clothes and scratching his skin. I put out my hand trying to grab him, and he reaches out to me.

Just as his fingers touch mine, one seems to come from nowhere and chomps down on his neck. He lets out a scream, his mouth forming an 'o' shape. A few of them are on top of him now, pulling him to the ground. I can hear his flesh ripping as they're tearing him to shreds. His organs are being pulled out from his stomach and I can see them eating his intestines. He looks up at me, and I can see the agony and panic in his eyes, but I can't do anything. It's too late. I hope he understands that, and can see the desperation in my eyes as his life slips away from him.

# TWENTY-FIVE

I can't move. I can’t speak. I don't even feel anything, just numb shock. Jake is dead. If I look down I can see his remains, his hair, his clothes, his bones, his blood. So I keep looking forward. Jake, who only last night I was imagining my future with. The man who I've lusted after for months at work, which I've only just really gotten to know. He's just gone.

The worst part of it all is the fact that I've failed. My one and only mission was to get him to his son. Now he'll never know what has happened to them. They'll never know what happened to him. No, I can't let that happen. I'm going to have to track them down, let them know. I'll tell them he was desperate to find them. That he did so much—that he died heroically. They have to find out.

The only problem is, I can't even move. I'm certain that the second I step down from this tree, I'll die. I already knew I couldn't do this alone, and now here I am. No one left to protect me. Only myself to rely on. I'm absolutely screwed.

Once the infected demolished Jake, they hung around under the tree for a while, feebly trying to reach for me. I kept silent and unmoving, but I know they could still smell me. Some were distracted by passing animals. It turns out they *are* eating them. Just another little snack for the things that have ruined my life. Eventually a fire broke out in a barn in the next field. I have no idea what caused it, or even what's going on over there. I don't care. I'm just glad that the chaos drew the rest of them away.

If I'm going to move, now is the time. If I wait much longer the infected will be back. I can get this much through my foggy brain. It's just hard to be productive when you're grieving. I don't really want to end up stuck here, starving to death until I drop down into their willing arms. If I just focus on one small task at a time, I might be able to get away from here. That's what Jake would do. I really don't think he would want me to just sit here waiting to be rescued by someone who is never coming.

Suddenly something just snaps inside me. A blinding blackout rage. Luckily this time, I don't scream, probably because there's no one to listen. I'm really frustrated at this whole situation. How dare this infection be unleashed on the human race? If someone has cooked it up, they deserve to die, and then go to hell. If the government is behind all this, then they're more evil than I could have ever imagined. I wonder if it has all gone to plan. If this is what they actually wanted to happen. Look at all these people suffering because of AM13. Look at all the lives it has torn apart. Look at everyone it's killed.

God, why did we have to come out here into this?

Why didn't we just keep our conversations and plans hypothetical? Everyone talks the big talk all the time about things they're going to do—quit their jobs, travel the world, break up with someone. But no one ever acts on it. It's just talk, and that's exactly the level we should have stayed at. We had to go ahead and follow through, well just look how that turned out. No wonder no one ever does anything.

I jump down from the tree, full of determination, and spot Jake's bag. I grab it, knowing he has more food than I do. I see that familiar glint of metal inside. The gun. Damn, if only he'd had it out, he might have been able to save himself. I know it would have been noisy, but we could have figured that out together afterwards. I decide to keep the gun firmly in hand. I have no idea how to use the thing, but I recon it's just one of those instinctive things, that when your life is in the balance, it just comes to you.

I start walking, in the opposite direction to the barn. I still have no interest in it. I just hope the fire kills the bastards that murdered Jake. I keep alongside the road, like we have done before, trying to pretend everything is the same, that I'm not more alone that I've ever been before in my whole life. The adrenaline rush from earlier is petering out and is being replace by fear. I don't know how to be decisive, how to figure out where to go and where to sleep.

...

The darkness is setting in and I'm so, so frightened. I still haven't found anywhere suitable. I've passed small villages, but I've not been brave enough to walk through them. I'm starting to think that's the only option I have left.

I keep going and going until I can walk no more. The pain in my legs is excruciating. I need to stop. I really don't want to, every moment I'm still is time where I'm vulnerable, but I have to. I can see a small wooded area with big warning signs at the entrance. My brain is telling me to avoid the place at all costs, but something is drawing me in. The signs don't worry me, what with crazy health and safety rules these days. I don't think I'll come across anything in there. From what I have seen, the infected stay in populated areas, and the authorities will never waste their time looking here.

I try to creep as quietly as possible, just to be careful, but all the twigs snapping and leaves rustling is making me stand out like a sore thumb. I'm sure if there are any infected in here, I'll hear them pretty quickly, but then, they'll hear me too. It's almost pitch-black now so I'm struggling to see what I'm doing. If only I had Michelle and Jake here.

I spot a light, out in the distance. It must be some kind of building. My heart starts racing again. I don't know how I feel about it, whether it'll be a good thing or not. Even though I'm totally alone, and there could be something bad in there, I have to check it out. It could provide me with a warm, safer night. I'm a bit surprised that there is a building in here, considering all the warning signs I saw. I knew there was no real danger.

When I get closer, I realise it's quite a big building, almost like the clothing warehouse we stayed at. What sort of business would be based out here? Maybe it's drugs. It must be something illegal. That thought doesn't stop me. To be honest, after everything I've been through, sleeping in a drugs den is the least of my worries.

The door swings open easily, too easily. I'm very wary, sure someone or something is about to jump out at me. I grip the gun tightly, waiting for the clarity on how to use it to flood through me, but nothing happens. Just ahead of me is another door, leading into the main room of the building I guess. Now is the time to be really quiet. I know I could just sleep here, in the entrance. I'm inside after all, but I'd never be able to shut my eyes not knowing what was on the other side. I'd never be able to relax.

The light streams through as I push the door open slowly. I stand back, aware of how loud my breathing is. I edge forward and pop my head around the door. The sight that greets me makes it feel like my heart has stopped forever.

# TWENTY-SIX

Infected. Everywhere I look. But I don't panic, they can't get to me. They're all in cages, like lab rats.

When my senses start to return to me, all I want to do is run, fast. I want to get as far away from here as possible, and to try and forget I ever saw this place. I don't though, because the larger part of me needs to know what the hell is going on here. It must be the news researcher in me. My finger tips are tingling. My whole body is fizzing with anticipation. This place is important. I can just feel it. Maybe it's a testing centre, to try and find a cure. Or maybe it's where the virus was created, where this chaos all began. I remember hearing it was started in Mexico somewhere, but that might not be true. Someone could have leaked that information to divert attention away from the real story.

I wander around the room, without even feeling my feet touch the ground. The eyes of the infected are boring into me. Some try to reach for me, snarling, but most are in such a horrid state that they can't even move. Some are so thin, they're practically just bones, and a lot of them don't have all their body parts. These ones are just rotting away, festering in a filthy cage. I wonder if they were bitten, or given the infection in this weird lab. This place is disgusting. No wonder the government were all for the lockdown, if this place had been discovered, there would have been riots.

I feel sick to my stomach, but more than that, I feel incredibly sad. These things might be cannibalistic monsters, but they used to be ordinary people. Now they have even been spared the right to a dignified death. Something has made them like this, they didn't choose it. No one would. Now to make things even worse, they're trapped here, unable to escape their cages. No one deserves this. No one.

I turn to leave. I can't even think about staying anywhere near this place. This is what hell must look like. I wish I was able to do something, to put them out of their misery, but I can't. I can't kill them all, I only have a gun that I don't even know how to use, plus it'd attract far too much attention. As I reach the door, eager to get some fresh air in my lungs, I hear a voice. A real human voice. I must be hearing things, any humans in this building would work here, and they wouldn't talk to me, they'd kill me before I could tell anyone about this place.

"Hey," the voice continues. I swing round, just to check. The voice sounds like Jake. I know that's impossible, he's gone, but that's too hard to ignore. The voice continues, getting more and more insistent. I scan the room, starting to feel uneasy. Then I see him, right at the back of the room, partially hidden by the other cages. A man, caged, but very much alive.

I rush over to him, excited that I can find out the truth about this place. Then it strikes me, he's caged which must mean infected. He's coherent, which is unusual but he must be very freshly bitten.

"Hi," I simply whisper to him. His eyes are pleading with me. They're so human, so full of life. I search his whole body, and can't instantly see any injuries, but that still doesn't fully convince me.

He talks quickly, and nonstop. It's as if he thinks a conversation will stop me leaving. "I’ve been here so long. It wasn't just me, not at first. I was with three other people, but when we got caught, they all got killed on sight." I raise my eyebrow at him suspiciously. "I was bundled into a van and bought here and I've been here for a few days, I'm not exactly sure how long."

"Why weren't you killed?" Something about his story doesn't quite add up.

"I don't know why, I've been asking myself that question ever since. I've been asking the scientists that work here that question, but no one will talk to me. They treat me as if I don't even exist." He looks down at his feet. "Maybe I'm just a test subject."

"Right, so what is it they're doing here? What are you a possible test subject for?" I'm hoping he may have overheard something.

"I really don't know. I *hope* they're looking for a cure." He smiles at me, and the desperation in his eyes is evident. He is silent for a few moments, before he starts begging. "Please, please help me. Please let me out of here, I'm going crazy. This is a nightmare; they're going to end up killing me." I stay silent, unsure. "I'll do anything for you, I promise. I'll take you to wherever you're going. I'll help you get food and water, whatever you want. Please. I can't stand this uncertainty, the waiting. I'm going insane I just want my freedom back. You have to understand. Please?"

I don't know what to do. I have no idea who this man is, or what he's capable of. I also don't know for sure that he doesn't have the virus. Plus the thought of another man accompanying me feels like a betrayal to Jake's memory. But the thought of company, of someone else to rely on, someone to help me, to protect me...It feels like the best offer I've ever heard.

He sits silently, while I consider all the options, before making my decision. He can see the confusion in my eyes. He must be able to see me wavering. Time passes while I think, struggling.

It's his silence that in the end makes the decision easy. He doesn't pressure me, continuing to beg until I can think no more. He actually respects my fears about him.

"Yes." I whisper and his eyes light up. "You can come with me, *but* you must do exactly as I say at all time." I want to regain some control over the situation.

"Oh thank you, thank you, thank y—"

I hold my hand up to silence him. "I need to get out of this hell hole now, it's driving me nuts."

He instructs me on how to release him. "It's all

activated by that set of switches over there." My eyes follow where he's pointing, all the time worrying. "Normally, it's controlled by finger prints, but it can be overridden by a key, which is kept in the second drawer down on the desk."

I'm impressed by his observations. Once the key is in my shaking hand, I move carefully. One false move and I fear everything in sight will be free.

As I'm unlocking the system, I concentrate hard. The guy constantly talks. He must be a nervous chatter. The only thing I pick up is his name, Mike. The rest is all buzzing, getting on my nerves and distracting me.

Finally, I've done it.

Red lights, flashing. Alarms sounding. Panic. Fear. What have I done? This must be bad, really bad. I can hear a screaming noise, where is it coming from? I look around, all the cages are opening. They're coming out. This is it. Oh my God, I need to run. It's then I notice the screams are coming from me.

Time stands still. Everything has been so quiet for days, so the loud alarm noise feels like an intrusion on my brain, my thoughts. I can't get myself together enough to do something to stop it.

I turn and run, towards Mike. My plan was to rescue him and that's what I need to do. Then I realise I don't even know this guy. Loyalties forgotten, I move towards getting the hell out of there. I grab my bag and get to the door. The gun, I forgot to pick it up. I look back to see my chances of retrieving it, but there's no hope. The infected are everywhere, shambling towards me. I need to move right now.

I yank on the door, and just as I'm about to hot foot out of there, I feel the unmistakable rushing poker hot pain of teeth clamping down on my shoulder.

# TWENTY-SEVEN

I instantly stop fighting, stop running my fate already accepted. I knew this journey would come down to this, the second Michelle vanished. I knew there was no chance of this having a happy ending, for any of us. Now that this has happened to me, I almost feel a relief. I don't have to feel guilty about being the last survivor. I don't have to pretend to be brave anymore. I don't have to go on fighting this exhaustion. The pain is radiating through my body. I'm so hot; sweat must be dripping from everywhere. My head feels funny, almost like my brain is starting to shut down already. If only we hadn't started this mission, if only we'd stayed in and worked like good little employees, if only.

Mike has pulled me outside, I don't even realise until the cold air slaps me in the face.

"But, you shouldn't. I can't," I try to tell him, try to explain. I need to make him run as far away from me as possible. I need to let him know that he's in danger being anywhere near me. I'm tainted, infected. If he stays, he'll have to kill me before I kill him. He's still pulling me, so I run with the motion. Even though I know he shouldn't be near me, I need to get him away from all of them more. They're coming, I can sense them. The sensation makes my skin crawl and my throat constrict. The alarms and commotion will attract more of them as well. Then he'll have no hope of escaping. At least I've still got enough brain power about me to talk to him, and I can force him to leave me, as soon as we get away from this nightmare.

I can't breathe. My legs are killing me. We've been running for ages. I want to stop, but I can't. I need to save Mike, and if I stop, he will too. After all the damage I've caused everyone else, including myself, this can be my one redeeming act, before I'm gone. God, I'm dreading becoming like that. A shuffling, moaning cannibal. I feel sick at the idea. I really wish I still had the gun, then I could kill myself before I have the chance to do any real damage. I don't have full confidence that I would be brave enough to pull that trigger though.

The bite hurts, but the pain is starting to ease off. I don't know if that's a good thing or a really, really bad thing. It could mean I'm losing myself already.

When we eventually stop, I fall to the ground, devastated. I want to cry, but the tears don't come.

"No, no, no, no," I repeat over and over. The shock is wearing off, reality finally hitting.

Mike interrupts my thoughts. "What's the matter? What's wrong?" I point to my shoulder and he pulls my top to one side to have a look. "Oh, that looks nasty. Do you have anything in your bag?" He pulls away to have a look.

The tears give up and roll down my cheeks at this point. "I'm so stupid. How could I have let myself get bitten? In that creep show circus of all places."

"Wait, what do you mean?" I look up at Mike's confused face. "It isn't a bite, it's just a cut. I don't know how you did it, it was all pretty chaotic." He laughs. "Don't worry. You're not going to turn into one of those freaks."

I'm so confused, and extremely tired. I can't get my head around the fact that I'm not going to die, after all that. Mike patched me up the best he could considering the minimal supplies I have left. I haven't decided if I trust Mike yet, but right now, I'm too tired to think. We sleep under a hedge, by the road far away from those evil woods. I hate to think what we've let loose on that place and any nearby town. I just hope everyone within the vicinity is following the lockdown. I black out too quickly to think about the cold and the dangers of where we are.

...

The first thing I see when I open my eyes is Mike. He's stood over me watching me sleep. I'm immediately creeped out. All I can focus on are his deep dark eyes. The eyes of a killer, I can't help but think as I sit up quickly. He starts talking to me, a jolly undertone in his voice, but all I can think about is how I need to get away from him, which is ironic considering the only reason he's here is because I wanted someone to look after me. Now I think I need to ditch him to save myself. I'm not sure what it is about him, I guess after all I've been through I don't actually trust the unknown. This guy could be some kind of weirdo, a pervert, a rapist, or a serial killer for all I know. We all know terrible situations like this can bring the worst out in people.

He gathers up all my things, offering to carry them for me to help me out, because I'm injured. I agree, grateful to not have to lug around that heavy load, but a small voice in my brain is yelling that he just wants to make sure I'm dependant on him so I don't go off alone. I don't know why I think this really, he's not given me any definitive reason. It could just be the paranoid voices in my head speaking, encouraging the gnawing feeling of unease in my stomach.

We walk, me slightly behind him, listening to him talk. I occasionally chip in with an "hmmm" or "yeah" just to keep the conversation flowing while I try and plan out my next move. My mind is whirring faster than it has ever gone. I feel wide-eyed and crazy. I wonder if I should just ask for my stuff and tell him to go, but a black cloud over my head is stopping me. I don't know anything about how dangerous this guy could be.

I just need to get home now. That's what this journey is about, and I won't feel safe at all until I'm back with my family. I wonder if they know that I've left the office. They might have phoned when they couldn't get through to my mobile and someone, maybe Jamie would have told them. I hope they're not too worried. I know they will be though, how could they not. I'm worried about them and as far as I know they're safely locked indoors. I bet Felix is seriously pissed off with me. We promised to keep each other updated on our situations and I didn't tell him anything about this. I'm sure he'll understand when I see him. I can explain it all to him then. He'll have to forgive me when I tell him how many times I nearly died. It'll be cruel to shout at me after all this.

I suddenly realise I've been constantly scratching the cut on my shoulder. That's weird, I hope it isn't infected. I've been so worried that I've been given AM13, what if it's tetanus or something? That would just be bloody typical of my life. In all this going on, I'll be the one to die of some illness that's been around for years. Maybe it's some kind of karma coming to bite me on the arse.

# TWENTY-EIGHT

We finally come across some public toilets, right on the side of the road. They must have been put there for tourists on long journeys. I tell Mike I'm going in. In these conditions, I'm not about to miss a chance to use proper facilities. He goes in to check it's all clear before I set foot in there, which is actually quite a nice gesture, yet all I can think is this is my chance to leg it. I would if he didn't have all my stuff. Damn, I really need to get it back. I have to, I can't survive without anything. I'm really on edge, bouncing from foot to foot. Mike might make me nervous, but it's worse being out here, alone, exposed with nothing to protect myself.

When I see his face again, I'm overwhelmed with a sense of revulsion. He looks dreadful; dark bloodshot eyes, messy, sweaty, and dirty. I'm sure I look just as awful, but there's something different about him, which I can't put my finger on. When he smiles to let me know all is safe, I force a grimace back. His teeth are blackened and it looks like his gums have been bleeding.

I dash inside and immediately whip my top off. There's a very dirty mirror, which I attempt to use to get a glimpse of my shoulder. The wound is revolting. It smells really disgusting and is all bruised yellow and purple. It really doesn't look like a cut, but then, I don't think it looks like a bite either. It's still really bloody, even after all the cleaning we did. Something isn't right about this. I need to see a doctor and soon, before it gets even worse. I need some antibiotics or something, to ward off infection or blood poisoning. As soon as I get home I'm going to try and get into a hospital. There must be somewhere you can go. I imagine they'll have had to keep some kind of medical facility up and running.

I start the tap running so I can splash some cold water on my face. I just need something to refresh me, while I come up with a miracle plan, but the water that runs out of the tap is just brown sludge. I thought they were going to keep water facilities running as normal? Maybe there's no need in these little toilets. I wish now more than ever that I was inside somewhere, safe. With TV and water and a warm bed. I'd give anything right now for a cup of tea and a hot meal. I'd eat literally anything right about now; even those vile meat balls from the other day seem appealing.

When I have stopped mooning over everything I haven't got, I get moving. Mike is still stood outside, in exactly the same position he was when I went in. He's staring into space, silent, and the expression on his face makes me feel icy and hollow inside. There is no way this guy is normal. He's just not right. It could be some kind of post-traumatic stress; after all, I have no idea how that affects people. I just feel like it's something much more sinister than that. I try and compose myself so he doesn't notice my negative attitude towards him.

...

We walk and walk and walk, sandwiched between a road and a train line. I'm just finishing up telling Mike everything about my journey so far, trying to keep it all friendly between us. I don't want him to suspect that I want to escape. "Keeping hidden is vital, obviously from the infected, but also the authorities—oh, but of course you already know that!"

My hint works, he takes over the conversation telling me about his own travels. "Yes. The three people I was with, the ones I mentioned before, well they were my girlfriend Maya and her younger sisters. We were actually on the way to their parents' house when we were caught." He stops for a moment, taking in a deep breath. "We all lived together, in university housing. Her sisters were a year younger than her, twins." He picks up on my confusion. "Obviously we'd heard about AM13, but didn't take too much notice. I don't think anybody did at first." I don't tell him anything about my original discovery of the video, even though this is the perfect time to. "Then, two days after the lockdown had started, one of the other guys we lived with came home looking as if he'd been beaten to a pulp, and acting crazy. Maya phoned the police immediately, while he trashed up the house in a rage.

Totally out of character for him. The operator on the phone got all panicky and ending up telling us to leave immediately, try and find somewhere else to stay for the time being, while they got someone to the scene to sort it all out. As we were rushing out, one of the twins got the message that their mother was in labour, so we decided to head there."

"Wow." I don't know what to say. I already know this story has a tragic ending.

"Yeah, so we quickly came across a police riot van and waved it down. We were actually relieved to see them—thought they would help us. The officer just got out of his van and shot the three girls without even looking at them." He tries to disguise the break in his voice with disgust, but the emotion is just too raw. "I was screaming at them, well, you can imagine. I don't know how they overpowered me, but before I knew it, I was in the back of the van, and it was taking me to that...place."

I feel terrible. He has been through so much more than me. He witnessed his girlfriend and her sisters' murder, and then he was forced into a cage, to have all sorts done to him. All I've been doing is judging him and assuming the worst.

"I don't remember too much after that." He surprises me when he continues. "I was in that cage, watching the scientists bringing in infected all the time and locking them up. I thought some of them were healthy, like me, at first, but it wasn't long before they turned as well. I kept thinking to myself that I would be next, that somewhere along the line I'd been given the virus, but here I am so I guess I was wrong. That's one good thing, I suppose."

"Maybe you were the control." Surely he wouldn't have survived this long if he'd been given AM13 somehow.

"Possibly. They took a lot of blood samples from me, but they did from everyone. I talked to them all the time. I was constantly asking them what they were doing, why I was there, but never got even a smile back." He shudders as he remembers the horrors. I wonder what all the scientists are going to think when they get into work tomorrow and the entire place is empty. That's if they don't get attacked on the way. It'd serve them right after the way they treated Mike. "I'd actually given up hope of ever surviving, I knew I'd seen too much, but then you came along to light up my life."

As he laughs at his joke, I find myself warming to him, and not just because of his compliments.

We find somewhere to rest, another night outside. I don't relish the idea, but we've walked miles today and I haven't seen anywhere suitable. We sit down to eat, and I open a can of beef curry, it smells mouth-watering. It seems crazy to me now that I was vegetarian. All I seem to crave is meat, so obviously my body needs it.

# TWENTY-NINE

The next couple of days are just endless walking. Everything hurts, even my lungs. Jake's estimations of how long this journey was going to take seem way off. I have no idea exactly how long I've been going, but it feels a lot longer than five days. We don't come close to any infected, but see hundreds. I'm sure they're multiplying rapidly as the days go on, but I'm not sure how unless they've stopped the lockdown. That's a scary thought. We don't seem to attract any attention, which means we can just carry on at a normal pace. We must be just outside of their radar of sound and smell. I wonder how long it'd take them to die out naturally.

We spend all our nights sleeping outside now. Trying to find a place to stay inside just seems too stressful, and considering we aren't really being bothered by the infected or the authorities, who clearly aren't doing their job of cleaning up the mess like they are supposed to, it seems pointless. Maybe we are getting sloppy. Hopefully this won't be our downfall. I actually manage to sleep really well, in fact I almost blackout. No thoughts swirling around in my brain, keeping it active, no constant shivering from the cold. My body must be acclimatising to these conditions, finally. Mike and I are just stumbling along through this journey together. He's actually becoming quite a good companion. I find myself thinking that I'm glad I rescued him.

I'm constantly tired these days. Way more than before. I'm not sure if it's the emotional upheaval, the grieving or simply the sheer amount of walking. When we're forced to pass through towns, I find myself staring aimlessly into shop windows, trying to keep a grasp on reality, on my old life. I try to think and behave like I did before all this happened, but it just feels like a character, not connected to me in any way. Why was I so obsessed with pointless things? Stuff that has no use or point these days—fashion, gossip, the few pounds I wanted to lose. What a waste of time.

Mike seems to think we're getting closer to my parents' house. I should be the one to know this, but my eyes feel almost steamed up. I can't focus for long enough to figure out where I am. Damn fatigue. So I just follow him along, trusting. I feel obligated to ask Mike what his plans are after I reach my house. I know he isn't exactly going to carry on with his previous course of action. I even extend an offer to let him stay with us until this whole thing blows over. He laughs, almost sinisterly and says that's probably not the best idea for both of us. I wonder what he means by that.

...

During the endless silence, I think about Jake's family. I'm still determined to make sure they know what happened to him. They must be frantic with worry. I don't want Harry to grow up thinking his dad just forgot about him, or didn't care, when he tried so hard to find them. That's not fair on him, or Jake's memory. I still blame myself for his death entirely, I can't help myself, and although I can never make up for it, I can at least do this.

Thinking about Jake brings with it a crippling sense of sadness. I will never ever get over what happened to him. It was so gory and brutal, the worst thing I've seen in my life. I always avoided watching horror films because I can't stand the sight of blood, and it was like watching my worst fear. His body tattered and shredded. Nothing left. I couldn't have even buried him if I wanted to. I can't help but think I could have really fallen in love with him.

I think back to the happier times we had together. I remember making such a fool out of myself in front of him, thinking he was never interested. Gossiping on the phone to anyone who would listen about what tactic to try next. That stupid email, the thing that I knew would end up ruining my life. Granted, I didn't think it would happen like this. Then that night, at the pub, our first kiss. How happy I was after, how full of promise it was. Getting closer to him as we met with Michelle to plan this God forsaken journey. The night at the petrol station...

Oh my God, the thought hits me so hard I stop dead still. Am I pregnant? Is that possible? I'm not sure, I don't know anything about babies, I've never had any interest in them at all. On the rare occasion someone has tried to talk to me about anything to do with the subject, I've always zoned out. Crazy emotions, meat cravings, tiredness, aren't they all supposed to be signs? I've got no idea and I'm really starting to panic. I don't remember using protection in my drunken haze. What an idiot. Stupid, stupid idiot. I can feel a sort of iciness in my spine; my blood has run so cold.

Mike's voice begins to penetrate my shock barrier. I didn't even realise I was mumbling to myself like an insane person. He sits me down and starts force feeding me water, trying to talk naturally to help me come round. I focus in on his eyes while he's talking, trying to find something real to concentrate on. What is with them? The irises are so dark. He just looks like a stereotypical evil crazy person. It must just be his ordeal messing him up; I've got to keep thinking that. He's the only person left I can trust, including myself. If I drive him away, I'll have no one and I'll never make it home, where I need to be now more than ever.

I start to explain to him my problem, in very basic detail, blushing as I tell him the tale. What a stupid thing to be embarrassed about considering. When he asks me where Jake is now I simply shake my head. The tears really start cascading down my cheeks. What have I done? I wouldn't know the first thing to do with a baby, especially one without a father.

Mike has gone off to get me a pregnancy test, to attempt to calm me down. He thinks he saw a pharmacy not too far back which will hopefully have something. I wish I'd asked him to get me something for my wound but I was distracted. It's so itchy now. I find myself scratching it constantly, even when I'm asleep. I really hope it's not something too serious.

I'm vaguely aware of all the infected wandering around, not too far away. They don't bother me anymore; I'm so used to their presence. Their disgusting, vile presence. Luckily they aren't too concerned with me either because I'd be no use fighting them off in this state.

# THIRTY

Negative.

The test is negative, but as I'm reading the instructions, it's hardly surprising. Apparently it won't show for a few weeks anyway. I can't stand that, I need to know *now*. How do people wait for weeks before they know either way? Doesn't the TV advert say they can tell you after one day of being pregnant or something? Surely technology has developed that far? I tear the page up, frustrated and annoyed with myself.

Now that the initial, irrational panic has subsided, I'm starting to see that there are many other reasons I could be experiencing the tiredness and crazy mood swings. After all, this isn't exactly a normal situation I am going through.

I have been getting a lot worse since I got the wound on my shoulder. I wonder if Mike knows more about it than he is letting on. I can't ask him, because he insists he didn't see anything, but wasn't he right behind me the entire time? I stay put for a while, out of Mike's sight and try and compose my thoughts. I just need to get through this day, get home, and then none of this will matter anymore. Luckily, Mike had the intuition to pick up pain killers and antibiotics from the pharmacy, so at least the trip wasn't in vain.

"I can't find out for sure yet, but it says negative." I shrug my shoulders, trying to seem unconcerned as I get closer to Mike. He nods, not knowing what to say. There isn't really anything he can say at this point. I smile back, hoping through the blur of medication I just took, it seems sincere.

We carry on, me trying to come across as if nothing has changed, as if I'm still treating him exactly the same. I just want to be with my family now, so desperately. I keep closing my eyes, hoping to open them and somehow, magically just be home.

Mike's chatter seems to be dwindling. Am I not responding adequately? I try and boost my end of the conversation, but now he's not really answering me so I fall into silence. I wonder what he's thinking. I try and think back over the day, to work out if I've done anything to make him suspect that I feel differently about him now. I can barely remember anything. How far have we walked? I don't even remember stopping for lunch like we normally do. I must have been in a daze. I guess after my shock today, it's only to be expected.

The next thing I'm aware of, we're settling down for the night. When did it get dark? I'm really disconcerted, but I guess I'm so used to the same routine by now, walking, eating, sleeping, walking, that I just tuned out. Similar to when you're driving, and your suddenly at your destination, but can't remember the journey.

There's a fire, Mike must have started it. What a dangerous move, that puts us right in view of anyone. Just as I'm about to say something, I see empty cans strewn around.

"Did we eat all that?" I ask indignantly. "That's just stupid, that's got to be all our food supplies gone!"

Mike laughs. "What do you mean? You ate all that, I only had that one. You just kind of went wild, eating so fast without stopping." He trails off when he sees my face. A range of strange emotions cross his face—confusion, denial, anger, and then a kind of smooth acceptance.

I have no idea what to make of all this. All I can really think about as I lie down is my itchy, itchy skin. So itchy.

...

The sun brings a strange kind of relief in the morning. I don't think I've slept at all, and I ache right down to my bones. I can't wait to get moving again because just lying here seems pointless, but first I need to eat, and I'm craving bacon badly.

Mike chatters animatedly as we walk, but he gets no response from me. I couldn't care less about a single word that comes out of that stupid guy's mouth. I think the pain in my joints, the lack of sleep and the constant starvation is making me cranky. Well, unfortunately for him, there's no one else to direct it at. I purposely ignore him, while keeping my eyes focused on my feet. I don't know how far we have got or even how long we have been walking for. All I can think about is I'm positive it must be time to eat again, I'm absolutely starving. I glance up, ready to tell Mike that I'm hungry so we're damn well stopping whatever he thinks, when I get a weird zinging sensation in my stomach. I must be hallucinating. I feel like I'm in some cartoon, where people turn into hot dogs or ice cream because you've let yourself get that hungry. The smell of him, it reminds me of pork.

I feel a hundred times better after food. I don't feel full, just less stressed. Mike says I'm hysterical when I'm angry, although for a split second he was terrified when he turned around to me, I looked that mad. I laugh weakly and tell him not to be ridiculous, I'm tiny, he could overpower me no problem.

While we were stopped, I decided to check on my wound. It feels like it's getting worse, not better. I've taken antibiotics and painkillers at every opportunity, too many really, just to keep it at bay until I can get home and find some help. Evidently this isn't working. It's revolting; puss-filled, leaking and still really, really bloody. It's fresh blood as well, not dried in and matted like I expected since I haven't been able to clean it properly. I caught Mike looking at it while it was exposed. He looked away quickly, but I caught the pity in his eyes. This made me feel so full of rage that I kind of let out a little growl, but at least I didn't hit the bastard.

...

Time is all starting to roll into one moment. We keep up the same routine without failure; walk, sleep, eat. What other choice do we have? I have no idea how long we've been going for. Sometimes, when the exhaustion really gets to me, I can't even remember where we're going. What all this is for.

Everything aches—my joints, my muscles, my organs. I'm acutely aware of every bone inside my body, rattling away, agonisingly. Mike doesn't talk. Sometimes I look up and I can't even see him. I don't panic though. I know he's there. I can still smell his stale rotten smell, so I just keep on walking. This must be what madness feels like. All consuming. Sometimes I want to laugh, but I know nothing is worth laughing at.

Food is starting to taste disgusting. The meat is rancid and doesn't quell any hunger. Everything I try tastes like cardboard crap. Then, with no warning at all, comes the rage. An overwhelming rage, I feel like I just want to tear everybody, and everything to shreds. Including myself.

When did I become like this? I must have cracked up somewhere, the pressure and grief must have pushed me over the edge. This must be what a breakdown feels like. I never thought I'd be one of those people who lose it, yet here I am. I must be crazy, what other explanation is there?

...

Itchy, so itchy. The itch has spread over my whole body. I can't even feel where the original wound is. It's an itch that I can't scratch. I can't stop thinking about this damn itch that I can't locate the source of.

Unlike Mike. He's gone.

I stop dead where I am. I don't know how I know it, but I'm just suddenly aware of the acute loneliness. I'm alone. Everything in my sight is crystal clear. I can see every dew drop on every blade of grass. But not Mike. No, not Mike.

# THIRTY-ONE

Mike. Mike. Mike. Every step I take, all I can hear is his name lodged into my brain. I can even taste him on my tongue. A sensation I know should be weird to me, but isn't. The fog has been lifted. I wasn't in my right mind earlier, that much I know. But that was preferable. I wish that crazy would take me again.

My skin is grey. It's been greying for days and I've been desperately trying to ignore it, trying not to notice the pus dripping down my back and the rotting smell that's becoming me. My mouth feels like sandpaper and my throat is raw. My insides are calling out for something, but I'm not sure what. Or more likely I'm trying to ignore it. If I can just make it home, I can get sorted. I can feel a pull in the right direction, so I know I'm going the correct way, without even lifting my eyes off the floor.

...

The moans of the infected are ringing in my ears. I'm sure they're all around me. In fact I'm positive they are. I try to recreate the fear that I felt before, just to connect myself to the earth, to who I was. Funny I should think of myself in that way, in the previous. I try to get my thoughts entirely focused on what I've lost and what I need to achieve. Faces swirling round in my mind, and me, trying to figure out who they are, and how I know them, but I can't.

A new noise. What is it? Car engines, I think. Hide? I'm not sure how to. I stop and wait for death, wait for the familiar sound of gun shots ringing out. Silence. A horrible long, ringing silence that seems to last forever. I lean back, and find a wall behind me and weep.

...

I open my eyes. When did I fall asleep? I have no idea where I am. A building. A school? My brain always takes a while to connect in the morning, especially when I'm in a new place, so this grogginess is comforting. But really, how did I end up here?

There are more infected than yesterday. I'm sure of it. Do I look so much like them now, that they totally ignore me? I try making a lot of noise, just to experiment. A very dangerous experiment. But nothing. A few glances, but I must be so dirty and gross now, I'm not even worth eating.

The next thing I'm aware of is ice cold running water, pouring over my head. Why am I standing here, under this gush, like my legs are made of lead? Maybe I thought it would be like a shower? But it's freezing, am I an idiot? Why can't I remember what lead me here? Is this a side effect of exhaustion?

I realise I'm dry again as I walk. I think I'm just walking as I don't know what else to do. This has been the sole purpose of my life for so long; I can't even remember what else I used to do. I can feel the pull again, deep in my stomach and I follow it because I know it'll lead me to where I've got to go. Walk, walk, walk. Others are walking alongside and behind me. Are they infected? I'm not really sure, I've become weirdly desensitised. I need to figure it out because either way, I could be in serious trouble.

I spot a girl, maybe six or seven years old. She has fallen over before me. I need to help her. That's what people do, help children, isn't it? Others are just stepping over her, ignoring her. I need to help. I try to pick up the pace and get to her before anything bad can happen. As I get nearer to her, I feel the familiar rage overtaking me. I'm angrier than I've ever been in my life. How can people just leave this sweet innocent girl like this? God the human race is fucked up. How can they leave her with infected wandering around everywhere, and how come all these people aren't indoors?

That's when I realise, with a sickening crunch, she hasn't fallen. Both her legs have broken. And not just broken, snapped off her body. And she's growling. Moaning and growling just like the others.

...

I look up. How long have I been asleep? Did I pass out? Did the sight of all that blood from a small innocent child cause me to faint? Was it her disconnected legs? The fact that she's infected? But no, I'm nowhere near where I was before. The sun is coming up; I must have simply gone to sleep. I'm relieved to have an explanation for my behaviour. I even smile to myself.

I suddenly hear a man, shouting, scared. Where is he? Is it Mike? I can help him. I can see him, I wave trying to get his attention, trying to separate myself from the rest, so he'll know I'm ok. I can't keep my arms up, they're too tired already. I decide to shout, but nothing but a low cry comes out. I haven't used my voice for so long, it must have gone. Or maybe it's because my throat is so damn dry.

He's running, running straight past me. He's ignoring me? But I can help him, I know I can. I can help him escape from these monsters, so he doesn't meet the same fate as the others. I run after him, as fast as my ailing body will let me. How can he run so fast? He's like lightening.

A moment later, I'm stopped dead in the road. Why did I stop running? Where is the man? That smell, it's so... I look down at the ground. There's about 20 infected, all tearing at something, and feasting. I need to get away from here before they notice me and I become the next meal. I just need to move.

But the smell, the smell draws me in. I can't remember the last time I ate, so I must be starving. I look closer, no longer scared, curiosity taking over. Is it an animal? Would that be so different from eating meat? Revulsion takes over me entirely when I realise it's him. That man. I recognise his green t-shirt. I didn't get to him in time. I didn't save him. They're eating him.

...

The next time I'm conscious, I'm alongside them, pulling out his intestines and organs and stuffing them into my mouth. I push myself back, disgusted in myself. I try to vomit but can only dry heave. What is happening to me? I'm revolting. I'm worse than the infected. They don't know what they're doing. I do. I'm nothing like them, so why was I behaving the same?

Walking again. I'm near home now. That thought bubbles up inside me, pushing everything else aside. Home. I don't know how I'll face my family after what I've become, but I can only hope they'll bring me back to myself. Familiar faces and surroundings. I won't be able to hide the massacre I've created. It'll be all over me.

...

I wake. I stand. I'm surrounded by them, hundreds it seems. They're all banging on a door. A building. The church. Huh? Seems weird to me. Why the church? What could possibly be here? Then, before I know it, I'm with them, hammering on the door. The smell of flesh too much to bear.

Suddenly, I'm at the end of the street. If I squint, I can see my parent's house. I walk until I'm there, at the door. I stand across the street, staring in the window. I'm weirdly uneasy, unsure of my next move. Do I try and get their attention or just walk forward and open the door, act normal as if this is just another day?

Before I can make a decision, Felix spots me. He stands up, distress etched across all of his features. He waves frantically and beckons me in, and my feet gladly obey. I realise now I didn't know how they would react to me and my appearance. I must look exactly like one of them. I'm absolutely covered in blood and I must be so dirty by now. It's so comforting to know that despite everything I've been through, everything I've done; my family will still accept me and help me heal.

I fall readily into my father's arms, relief and warmth rushing through me. I have never been so happy in my life. When he pulls me back to get a good look at me, the smile on my face is the biggest and brightest I can manage. I can see the worry in his eyes as he scans my face. It hits me hard what I must have put them through and I try and convey my apology in my expression. I know as soon as I open my mouth to talk the tears will start, and once I open that floodgate, it'll be a long time before it shuts again.

I tear myself away, desperate to see my mum. She's the only face I haven't looked at yet, and as soon as I do, all will be complete. My eyes finally meet hers and my instant thought is how much older she looks. Shock reverberates through me. My brain recollects a memory of her telling me she was unwell. How ill is she? Or is this all because of me and the stress I must have put her through? Happiness rapidly gives way to guilt as I move towards her, desperate to hold and comfort her.

She immediately backs away. I'm confused by her reaction, is she mad? She's never really been angry at me before; I've always done as I've been told, never given her any reason to yell. I continue to walk towards her until she ends up cowering against the wall, I can't understand what I've done to cause such an adverse reaction from her. She's actually trembling.

"Please. Stop." She whispers so quietly I can barely make out the words, but she may as well have screamed them for the pain they cause me. "I know what you are." I try and get closer, just so I can hear her better but she recoils so forcibly that I think better of it and just attempt to strain my ears. "I wish you weren't, you're my only daughter." She stops and tries to catch her breath. She flicks her eyes between dad and Felix. "We can all see it, just look at her. She's infected."

Dread shoots through me, my brain goes into overdrive. Now what? I can hear Felix defending me—I'm not surprised by this. He has spent his whole life sticking up for me. He's insisting that once I've had a wash, a sleep and a hot meal, I'll be back to my normal self. I notice my dad is silent. I glance up at him, knowing if I can just get him on my side too, mum will eventually have to come around. He's staring intently at me. I feel insecure under his gaze. I try and silently communicate with him that I'm fine, that I may have done bad things, but that doesn't make me a monster. I'll never be like them.

He moves forwards tentatively, his gaze never leaving mine. He holds my face in his hands for just a second before his fingers reach down to my shoulders. I tense, begging him in my mind not to look under my top, not there. As soon as they see that wound, they will immediately get the wrong idea. I hear a rip and close my eyes, preparing myself for what's about to come.

The hysteria is intense. My mum starts shrieking, a noise I never thought could have come from her small, frail body. She runs into the other room taking my last hope of survival with her. My dad starts shouting at Felix to get something, anything to 'take me out' before I can do any real damage. I look pleadingly at Felix, but even he has lost confidence in me, his stunned silence says it all. Nothing I can say or do now will change any of their minds.

I need to run.

I need to get as far away from this house as possible. Why did I even come in? I try and yank myself out of dad's grip, but he's so strong and holding on to me so tightly. He's mumbling an apology, an explanation to me. I don't want to hear it. He can't justify killing me, when there is nothing wrong with me, however much he seems to think it's 'for my own good'.

I attempt to block out his words, I really want to, but

he's determined I'm going to hear him. Agitation is slowly developing into rage, and the anger is blocking out every other emotion. How dare my family treat me in such a disgraceful way? I have done nothing bad to them; I don't deserve any of this. I want to scream in his face. I'm not one of those things. Violent thoughts swirl round and round in my brain until I'm not even sure what I'm doing any more.

I sink my teeth into my father's arm. I need to get him off me somehow. But I don't stop there, I can't. I find myself tearing all the flesh from his body and devouring it, an insatiable hunger that I didn't even know I had, completely controlling all of my actions. I can't stop, I know I should, I wish I could. Even though I know what I'm doing and I know it's wrong, I carry on.

I'm suddenly aware of a prickling sensation on the back of my neck. Someone is watching me. I snap my head up and see Felix. The terror in his eyes causes my heart to pound. I'm instantly ashamed. I stand up and look down at myself. I'm disgusting, maybe I am infected. Maybe I am just like those things. I have actually become one of the things I have been hiding away from for all this time.

I want to take it all back, I want things to be the way they were before any of this happened. I'm sorry, my loving brother must understand.

Then my eyes settle on the baseball bat in his hand and I remember what he was going to do to me, what he's still going to do to me, and I pounce on him, like an animal, without a second thought. Shock must have rendered him frozen because he doesn't even try to fight me off as I devour every inch of him, licking my lips and enjoying every bite. Sucking every bit of meat off his bones. What a weakling. At least dad struggled first.

I sniff the air, somehow understanding that my nose can help me find my mother. She's next. This is all her fault. She started this. If she could have just let me have a shower and sort myself out, none of this would have happened. Dad and Felix would still be here.

I can sense she's hiding behind the sofa; I can taste her fear on my tongue. I want to play a game with her. I want to make her suffer. I open my mouth to speak, to tease her a bit, to pretend that she isn't going to meet the same fate as the others, but to my frustration only a low growl passes through my lips.

I stalk quietly, moving slowly towards where she is. Her emotions are all heightened and she's sweaty. This causes her to smell more delicious than anything I've ever tasted. Anticipation and excitement tingles in my stomach as I wait, forcing myself to savour this moment. I move until she can see me and I snarl.

...

As I wander out of the house, I look down at the warm blood splattered across my hands and I grin to myself. I tortured mother for hours, eating little bits off of her now and again, not enough to kill her or even allow her to black out, just enough to ensure she was in agonising pain. It was terribly hard to keep control of myself, she tasted amazing, but I had to make her pay, she needed to understand what she's caused. I'm not sure if I truly got through to her because she spent the whole time screaming at me to get it over with, to kill her already, when she really should have been reflecting on her awful behaviour.

I was bored by the time she took her last breath, and glad to just finish my meal. Although, now I'm done, I'm not really sure what to do. What's next? There is no point in me going back inside, there isn't anything left for me there. I guess I just carry on walking, the same as before.

# About the Author

Samie Sands lives in a small seaside town in England with her husband and daughter. She has a degree in Media Studies and has spent her career working as a Graphic Designer. She enjoys reading books from all genres, particularly horror and spends far too much time with her head in a book. *Lockdown* is her debut novel.

Printed in Great Britain
by Amazon.co.uk, Ltd.,
Marston Gate.